§When the Wrong One§
Loves You

Who said, love, can't kill????

§ *When the Wrong One* § *Loves You*

A Novel

J. D. Willd

Published by Willd Ink

ISBN: 978-0615703879

First Edition

Published by Willd Ink

For my son, Alan

And

For the heavenly father

And

For all my friends and family

And

My mother, who inspired me every day

I will never forget you.

For my dear friend

Tammie Ward

§ *When the Wrong One* §
Loves You

§

The room was as cold as a winter morning in January, when the police forced their way in, hoping to find an empty apartment. What they found that day would live with them for the rest of their lives. The body was hanging upside down, tied to an old rusty box spring. All of the man's skin had been removed, along with his genitalia, and all of his blood was drained from his body.

This devious killer saved the worst for last. From inside the small one bedroom, the killer placed his handy work on display for the police and the world to admire. The apartment was pristine as clean as most hospitals, except for the body of the slain victim. Detective's Bradley Richards and Mike Reese found no evidence that anyone had been in the apartment. They knew all too well who was behind the death of this young man. The only question that remained is could they stop them before it happened again?

§ 1 §

The summer had been one of the hottest on record. It was a joyful and exciting one for David Williams and Benjamin Brown as the young couple was living the American dream. The closing of their new home was only three days away and David had already told everyone. The couple couldn't believe after six years of living in apartments and saving money they were about to fulfill a dream.

David had always wanted to have a home in the far west end of the city he loved; now he had one. The couple had been together since high school, but finding the money to live their dreams didn't come cheap in a city as diverse as Richmond. Most homes cost half a million dollars in the right neighborhoods. Benjamin, David's lover, had only been working for Verizon for about five years. The two met when they were seventeen and fell in love. They told no one about their relationship until after college.

David had been working with a local doctor, Dr. Anderson, since high school. David is the idea of young and handsome with long dirty-blond hair, big blue-green eyes, and a tall lean stature.

David, a native of Virginia, had always been just a little different from other guys. His feminine mannerisms and shy personality made it hard for him to fit in. Benjamin was the opposite; he could easily pass for a straight man without much effort. His charisma made him likable to most in school. Benjamin was just a little shorter than David but slender and well built. He had shoulder length dark hair and eyes to match David's.

Raised by his aunt and uncle, Benjamin found life difficult after his mother died from breast cancer. His father, who drank himself to death, never had much to do with Benjamin. Benjamin and his family moved from Texas when he was fifteen after his uncle received an offer from Verizon, known then as (Bell Atlantic).

Benjamin's uncle helped him get his start with Verizon after college. The move had been hard on Benjamin at first. Meeting David changed things for the better over time. David was from a very close family and found it hard to understand why Benjamin wasn't close to his own. With time, David would come to understand that not every family shared the close bond that his did. David had always been extra close to his older sister Sara. They had always shared everything with one another. David didn't tell Sara about his sexuality until he shared the news with their parents. Sara still held his secrecy against him even today.

Even though their families had never understood their relationship they did manage to remain open minded.

David's mother Amanda was the first in the family to see their new home, she had always been very involved in their lives and wanted to make sure that the guys had everything they needed.

Both young men loved Amanda, but one could safely say that she could be just a little overbearing sometimes. Benjamin's Aunt had stopped by several times herself offering to help. His Aunt persisted, regardless, of the guys telling her and David's mother that it wasn't necessary. The need for David's mother and Benjamin's Aunt to help had more to do with a never-ending need to outdo one another.

Things in their lives couldn't have been better. They had found their dream home and had started making it into something they both always wanted. The selling point for David was the tall white column's that surrounded the front of the house, while Benjamin was sold on the living space, 3600 square feet to be exact.

The four acres of land that surrounded the house was the main selling point for them both. The only problem the young lovers seemed to face was making time for each other. Making the home their own and adding desires to the home caused David and Benjamin to seem far from each other. David's friend Monica, who owned the little antique shop where he found most of the great pieces for his home, helped him locate everything he asked for over the next six months. Willow Antiques had become David's little home away from home while decorating. Benjamin had often voiced his anger over the money David spent furnish their home with all that he loved; after all, everyone knew that antiques didn't come cheap. Nonetheless, Benjamin himself found spending money just as easy when trying to make their new home everything they dreamed it could be. That became very clear to David when he found Benjamin had spent close to twelve grand having a new pool put in the backyard.

The couple had talked about putting one in someday, but David never thought Benjamin would spend that kind of money without talking to him first. After all, most of the money the two shared was David's in the first place.

This was a fact that often caused the couple to fight. David would always say whatever's mine, is yours. Nevertheless, Benjamin always found a way to make David feel just a little guilty about his family's wealth. David had worked hard all his life to make his own way in this world, and not once had he used his family's money for his own needs. Benjamin clearly didn't understand.

Once the couple completed their dream, they made plans to have their friends and family over for a housewarming party. The party would change many things in the couple's lives, not all of them would be for the better. As the planning began, David felt that they should have something small and simple, but Benjamin wanted something over the top. After all, Benjamin always said, "if it's worth doing it's worth doing right." After a week of fights and hurt feelings, David agreed to let Benjamin have his fun. The night of the party David's best friend Sean Wilson was the first to arrive. David's parents, Amanda and Charles, were the next to follow.

David had been best friends with Sean for almost twenty years, both having grown up in Richmond together. They quickly formed a lasting friendship after meeting in grade school.
Sean had never really cared for Benjamin, but you would never hear him say anything bad about him or anyone else. Sean was one of a dying breed of young men; you know the ones that have a kind heart that seems to show in everything they do.

David had always told everyone how lucky he was to have Sean in his life. Not everyone agreed that Sean was Mr. Perfect. In fact, Benjamin had often voiced his dislike for him. Amanda had often said that her son had fallen in love with the wrong man and she never failed to voice her opinion on the subject.

Then again…Amanda often voiced her opinion on everything she didn't like.

The party was everything Benjamin and David hoped it would be. Everyone seemed to be having a great time. However, the real party began after David's parents left for the night. They took with them the cold chill that had filled the room when his mother entered. David's father, Charles, was just the opposite. Everyone seemed to really enjoy his company. Yet, when Amanda say's it's time to go, no one ever says no.

That night David found out that his sister Sara had been dating a really nice young man by the name of Jason Haywood. The couple had been going out for six months and planned to marry at the end of March, which was only three months away. David was overjoyed for his sister, but he still felt that she was moving just a little fast. Even fast for her. He and Benjamin had never even talked about marriage before.

The party had started to die down as most of the guests had gathered in the couple's sitting room. Most of them had started sharing stories about their wild sex lives.

Even though David disliked such topics he found some of the stories a little wild and hard to resist. The stories were about the wild times the couples had been having thanks to some sex parties they attended around town after dark. The only thing that neither David nor Benjamin understood was how their friends learned about such parties.

Missy and Roberta explained that if you looked in the right places on the Internet you could find anything. Benjamin, always just a little wilder than David, started to smile at the thought of wild sex with a young hunk. David, on the other hand, seemed just a little taken back by the idea.

David's only dream since high school had been to marry Benjamin and live the best life possible. After hearing the stories their friends shared he wasn't sure that would ever happen. Roberta started talking about the first time she had gone to one of the parties. The story she shared made everyone in the room blush.

Roberta spoke of dog collars and thick dildos, hard dicks, the smell of sex and wet willing pussy, and the fingers that found their way into the young victims. She told us about the moans of pleasure coming from every room, and the nameless strangers meeting in passionate kisses. Roberta told us about her own heaving breast, and how the young slave found her round pink nipples and bit down cause great pain and pleasure. She told of the young lovers crying out "Yes, Oh God, Yes!" and everyone in the room wanted to be there if only in our minds.

David wasn't sure what to think about the wild act's Roberta was speaking of. Benjamin seemed more than willing to think about having sex with nameless strangers.

The very idea of sharing Benjamin with someone made poor David feel sick at his stomach. After all, he had been in love with the same man for fourteen years now.

After the party, Benjamin wanted to learn more about the world they just heard about. One could always say that Benjamin loved the idea of great sex, even when that sex didn't involve his lover. For now, David would have to learn to live with the idea of Benjamin wanting to play.

The weeks that followed were spent getting ready for Sara's wedding. While helping with his sister's wedding David to start thinking about his own dream of marrying Benjamin. Anytime he tried to share his feelings with Benjamin he would always change the subject saying he didn't want to talk about it.

That should have served as a warning to David that all was not as it seemed in their perfect little world. Yet, David never thought much of it other than Benjamin was not ready for marriage. However, the truth was that Benjamin had been having an affair with a young man named Cole for several months and without anyone suspecting a thing.

David really believed that Benjamin was working overtime so that they could replace some of the money the couple spent finishing their home. The truth was the long hours were so Benjamin could be with his lover. In the end, it was Amanda that discovered Benjamin had been playing the field. She witnessed him coming out of a local hotel with Cole.

One could never be sure what Amanda would do next since it was clear that she did not believe a word that had come out of Benjamin's mouth. David had always been Amanda's baby and the thought of someone hurting him really made her want to take vengeance against Benjamin. Sadly, she didn't want to be the one to break David's, heart. The one thing you could be sure of is that Amanda would make Benjamin pay from then on.

The days leading up to the big day for Sara were filled with last minute details. Amanda and the rest of the family had been working around the clock trying to make sure everything was perfect for Sara and Jason.

David still wished that he and Benjamin could at least talk someday about having a little ceremony of their own, but Benjamin refused to talk about it with him without being a total asshole. All that changed after Amanda found out his dirty little secret. It seemed that Benjamin had a major change of heart and that alone made David aware that something wasn't right. At the time, David didn't want to think about what he knew in his heart.

David walked the dark hallway trying to find the room where his sister was dressing only to make sure she had all she needed. "Hi," he said as he walked in finding Sara dressed and ready for the big moment. "Do you have everything that you need love," He asked. "Yes, I think so," she said with a little crack in her voice, "but a little help sure couldn't hurt." David could tell right away Sara was suffering from a bad case of the nerves.

The two had always been close and that day David felt like he was losing his best friend, but Sara quickly told him that he would never lose her to anyone. The two hugged one last time before their mother barged in taking over once again, as she always did. Benjamin was waiting outside of Sara's dressing room door as David came out and the two made their way downstairs for the ceremony.

Right before they walked into the crowded room filled with loved ones and friends from all over, Benjamin pulled David into his arms and asked him to marry him.
Although David knew what he wanted to say, he could not get the words out for some reason.

Benjamin was standing there with a smile on his face that read "I love you," but David knew something wasn't right about the whole thing. So, after what seemed like hours, he looked Benjamin in the eye and said I can't answer you right now. Please give me time to think about it.

Benjamin suddenly became upset saying "you love me or you don't, it's just that simple." "But Benjamin it's not that simple because I do love you, I'm just not sure I want to marry you right now," David said. Without another word he turned and walked away leaving Benjamin standing alone. The ceremony was perfect, Sara had never looked so lovely, and anyone could easily see the young couple loved each other.

The wedding was one of the most beautiful memories David had ever shared with his family or Benjamin. The hunger for something special made the day seem hurtful somehow, but with any luck that would all change soon.

Amanda found David standing alone in the corner of the room looking like someone had just killed his favorite pet. However, when she tried to ask what the matter was, he turned and walked away without a word. "David!" she called trying to get her son's attention, but it was no use. She could tell he did not want to talk about whatever was on his mind just yet, so she left him alone for the moment.

Benjamin walked over to see what was going on, but Amanda told him she did not feel a need to share her thoughts or feelings with the likes of him and walked away. Feeling like someone outside looking in, Benjamin decided it was time to leave the wedding before someone said something that would cause David to leave him for good. Benjamin searched everywhere for David only to find him sitting alone in a dark room. When he tried to talk, David told him they had nothing to really talk about unless he wished to tell him about the young man he had been sleeping with.

Benjamin suddenly came to life asking David, "Who told you about Cole?" Then David looked him in the eye and said, "You just did!"

As David walked out of the room Benjamin tried his best to stop him but found that he wasn't fast enough. After that, Benjamin knew that going home was a bad idea. He went to his aunt and uncles for the night. When his aunt Kay tried to ask if anything was wrong, Benjamin asked her to leave him alone so he could think. "Okay, my dear," she said and then turned to walk out of the room. Before she did, she looked at Benjamin and said, "Remember this, if you need me I'm here."

The next morning, as Benjamin enjoyed breakfast with his Aunt Kay and Uncle Ben, he asked them how they would feel about him and David having a little wedding at their home in a few months. And to his surprise, they both thought the idea was wonderful.

§ 2 §

When Benjamin arrived home that morning, he found that David was not alone, Sean was sitting next to him on their bed. And without a word, Benjamin made his way over and kissed him hard on the mouth. David quickly pulled away, asking him what he thought he was doing since he did not even bother coming home the night before.

But before Benjamin had a chance to really tell his side of the story, David asked that he leave him alone with his friend so that they could finish making plans for their night out on the town. Benjamin feeling the anger building inside, asked David when he thought he would be having his little night out? David looked up without missing a beat and said, "Tonight looks good;" after all, you spent last night out doing your thing.

And before Benjamin had a chance to say another word, David up and left the room.

The two young men would not talk again for the next three days, and when they did it turned into an all-out fight. Benjamin knew that he had done wrong by David, but he also knew that he loved him, and wanted to make a life with him now more than ever.

Although David found himself unable to really understand what had gone wrong, he knew that he was in love with Benjamin and that he wanted them to have a life together.

After nearly a week of fights, and hurt feelings, the guys had everything worked out or so they thought. However, what David didn't know wouldn't hurt him, Benjamin thought. Amanda stopped by one afternoon to make sure that her son was okay since she hadn't heard from David in a few days. David explained that everything was fine, but did tell her that he and Benjamin had been having a few problems.

Amanda asked if there was anything that she could do to help, but David quickly told her that it was okay, because he had everything under control.

Benjamin had really started taking the time to make sure that David knew that he loved him. He would send him flowers and take him to dinner at least once a week, and sometimes more, but their sex life had really fallen apart, in fact, they hardly had sex anymore. David had tried everything to make things better. But, that would all change when unexpectedly Benjamin asked David about having a little fun in their bedroom.

Although David wasn't sure what Benjamin had in mind, he knew that he wanted to make their love life strong again, so he asked about the idea. Well, Benjamin said, "I wanted to talk to you about us having a little three-way, with a cute guy I know from work." The look of shock on David's face told the whole story, and without a word, one could tell that he was anything but happy about the idea.

For weeks after, the couple did nothing but fight, mainly because David hated the idea of having someone that he did not know in bed with them; however, Benjamin could not see the harm in having a little fun. Maybe the idea of being faithful had never crossed Benjamin's mind, but David was the opposite because monogamy was all that he wanted.

David called the only person that he knew would give him an honest answer about the whole idea, and that was Sean his best friend.

Sean understood perfectly about the situation and did his best to help David see things from Benjamin's point of view. However, David was not happy with the fact that his best friend was on Benjamin's side on something that was so out of character for him. Even though in truth David would never understand Benjamin's, need to cheat.

Benjamin couldn't have been happier when David told him that they could give the three-way thing a try once, and see if everyone was okay from there. Benjamin called his little friend and asked him to stop by that night, only to find that he already had plans with someone else. Although Benjamin was a little disappointed that Cole had plans, he told him that they could get together another night soon.

However, their little three-way wouldn't take place for several nights. Cole let them know that he was free the next evening, but David had already made other plans.

That night David was out having dinner with his parents and Sean, while Benjamin was out having sex with a stranger. David arrived home that night to find Benjamin was once again missing in action, after telling him that he was not up to going out, and suddenly he knew that Benjamin was once again cheating.

Benjamin came home around one in the morning with the smell of alcohol and tobacco on his clothes, but David didn't say a word because he knew that the best thing to do was catch him in the act. David had always been the kind of young man that went out of his way to take care of the people he loved, but now all that seemed to leave him as he found himself thinking of ways that he could make Benjamin pay for hurting him.

Benjamin unaware that David was on to him started asking about the little three-way plan they had made a few days ago, and to his surprise, David once again said: "yes, let's have a little fun." Benjamin made all the arrangements with Cole. However, David asked if Cole could come around eight instead of nine. Benjamin was so overcome with happiness that he forgot to ask why David wanted to change the time.

David had already called his best friend Sean and asked that he show up at the same time, that way he would have a good reason not to go through with Benjamin's plans, but to his despair, Sean didn't show up that night. It had just turned eight o'clock when Cole arrived, but when David looked around for Sean; to his dismay, there was no sign of him anywhere. The night had started out on a bad note, but things would soon turn around for everyone. Cole was just as sexy as Benjamin had said he was, but he was also a very charming young man.

Cole's dark complexion and deep-set chestnut eyes really made it easy to see why anyone would enjoy having sex with such a beautiful young man.

David and Cole really hit it off, but for some reason, this did not seem to set well with Benjamin, who had been trying to get them apart all night, without much success.

David found himself lost in Cole's eyes as their lips met for their first kiss, and David let his hand find its way down to Cole's now throbbing basket. Their kiss lasted for what seemed like hours, and without a word the two got up and walked into the bedroom, leaving Benjamin sitting alone and angry as hell over the fact that his two lovers had left him completely out.

David and Cole were deep in the thralls of passion when Benjamin walked into the room. However, to his surprise neither David nor Cole looked up as he entered the room. The two young men seemed lost in their lovemaking, as their moans of pleasure well indicated. Benjamin was truly beside himself, as the two men that he had always thought would hate each other, were now having wild sex without him. Once David saw Benjamin watching them from beside the bed, he motioned Cole to pull out of him, and without a word, Benjamin eased himself onto the bed. And without moving an inch, David slid his rock hard manhood into Benjamin causing him to cry.

Cole wasted no time in getting behind David and doing the same, and as David felt his thick manhood entering him yet again, he knew that he and Cole would see each other again. The night came to an explosive end with all three young men climaxing at the same time. Once Cole had gone that night David knew, that Benjamin had been unhappy about the fact that they had really liked each other.

However, he also knew that Benjamin would never say a word for fear that David would know that Cole was his lover.
The next day David called Sean to find out what happened to him the night before, but to his surprise, Sean told him that he had called to cancel their plans. "What do you mean, I called and canceled," he asked? "I mean you called and left a message that said you had changed your mind and wanted to go through with the three-way with Benjamin". "Well", David said, "looks like Benjamin has outsmarted us once again, but this time it just might work out better for us in the end".

"What do you mean", Sean asked? "What I mean is that Cole and I really had great connection last night, and poor Benjamin, really felt left out. I actually felt sorry for him for about a minute or maybe two".
"You are bad, you know". "Yes, I know, but you love me anyway", David said with a smile. "Yes", Sean said with the same smile on his lips, "but really, what are you thinking about doing with that young man Cole is it"? "Yes, his name is Cole, and as for what I am going to do with him, maybe it is better if you do not know", David said. "Well, why do you say that love" "after all, I know everything about you", Sean said.

"Well, maybe you do, and maybe you don't, my dear, after all, a guy has to keep something's to himself", David said with the same sweet smile. That afternoon as the two said their goodbyes;

David knew that if he ever wanted to make Benjamin pay for his little sleep around all he had to do is call Sean.

Everyone had known for the longest time that Sean was in love with David, but poor Sean would never let anyone know, for fear of him finding out. David had other plans for young Cole, after all, Benjamin thought he could sleep around and never get caught, well he was wrong, not only was he caught, but he was also about to lose his lover.

It didn't take long for Cole to call David to see about meeting again, but David was just a little shy about cheating at first, but soon realized that it was the only way to get what he wanted and that was to keep Benjamin.

David and Cole had started meeting at least three or four times a week, but David had made it a point to tell no one about his plans. Cole was everything you could hope to find in a lover, hot, sexy and always ready.

Although David understood why he shouldn't feel bad about cheating on Benjamin, something inside still felt wrong. The weeks passed and still Benjamin said nothing about what they had shared with Cole the night of the three-way; however, David wasn't all that surprised since Benjamin didn't want him finding out about his little affair.

The weeks passed by like flashes of lightning, and David found himself still enjoying his little sex games with Cole.
Benjamin had all but given up on his little cheating fest with Cole, after finding it almost impossible to find time alone with him.

§ 3 §

After weeks of avoiding it, Benjamin asked David if they could finally talk about the night they spent with Cole. However, before he had a chance to finish his thought, David jumped in, with its okay, I already know what you are going to say and I understand.

Feeling angry Benjamin jumped up and said, "No it's not alright, we need to talk about what happened even if you don't want too". As David turned around to have a seat, he saw the sadness in Benjamin's eyes and knew that he was hurt, by his own actions. While David understood why Benjamin had been so upset by what he had done, he also knew that he still loved him with all his heart. As they talked that night David found himself feeling guiltier than ever for having an affair with Cole behind Benjamin's back.

However, he also knew that by having his little affair, the man he loved had come back to him once again. Benjamin and David vowed to never let anyone or anything come between them again. That night they made love for the first time in almost two months, and the passion that was once there came again full force. David lay next to Benjamin that night knowing that his affair with Cole was about to end; however, instead of feeling upset, he felt a sense of peace come over him.

The next day David met Sean for lunch and the two of them talked about all that had just happened between himself and Benjamin, but the words that Sean spoke that day filled David with fear. What if the whole I am sorry baby, thing is just a ploy to get you back into his bed again, Sean asked? The look of shock that came to David's face must have shown through because Sean was quickly telling him that he didn't mean to upset him.

However, David stopped him, and said: "baby you didn't upset me because I have already thought of that one myself." Sean had always known that David was smart, but this time he even caught him off guard.

Sometimes when you love someone you have to give him or her enough rope, so that they can hang themselves in the end. But, in this case, I pray that I am wrong about Benjamin.

As the two finished their lunch David told Sean all about his plans to keep things on track with Benjamin. But deep inside, he hoped that his plan worked. Sean had always been a great friend to David, but lately, he seemed more concerned with why he should leave Benjamin as opposed to staying and making it work.

Sean had never really had a long-term relationship of his own so to speak, but he had always given David great advice in the past about how to make things work with Benjamin, so his new attitude really took him by surprise.

But David told himself it was just Sean's way of looking out for him.

Weeks passed and David found himself falling deeper in love with Benjamin every day. The two of them had really started making things right again, much like they were when they first fell in love. However, the couple soon found themselves going down the same old road, working too much and not paying attention to one another. But, David had a plan this time that he knew would keep the home fires burning. It was late one Thursday night when the couple was laying in bed. David turned to Benjamin and asked if he had ever thought about what their friends said during their housewarming party? Benjamin feeling just a little shocked by what David had just said, took a few moments before he said, "yes, I remember, why?" However, David wasted no time explaining his idea. And once the couple had a chance to talk about it they both agreed to give it a try. David remembered what everyone said that night about how you could find anything you wanted all anyone had to do was look, and they were right. David found just what they were looking for right away. The next night a young couple from Richmond was hosting an open party that was guaranteed to fulfill anyone's dreams. After reading the ad several more times, David knew that the party was just what they needed and he printed the article. David grabbed it from the printer and ran to the bedroom to show Benjamin.

At once Benjamin began to smile saying "this sounds like a wild time" maybe because the ad read (come one, come all, to the wildest sex party on earth, 9 pm. Friday.) After the couple talked about what being at the party would feel like for the better part of an hour, they fell asleep. That night as David lay asleep in Benjamin's arms he began to dream about all the possibilities that awaited them at the party, and who they might meet when Cole came to mind.

Would he be there David wondered, or would there be men as sexy just waiting to make his dreams come true? Either way, David couldn't help but see visions of hot men all wanting to have their way with him, and Benjamin. The next morning as the young men prepared for work David found himself looking at the clock repeatedly.

Hoping that the day would pass quickly so that the visions in his head would stop, but time didn't seem to understand his need for the night, as it was moving as though it were standing still. However, when the day finally did end, David found himself getting a really bad case of cold feet. But Benjamin started explaining that the party could open up so many doors in their relationship if only David would open his mind to the idea of having fun. Although David didn't seem that happy about what Benjamin had said, he still agreed to at least give the party a try. Thankfully, as the couple arrived, a sexy young man wearing only a smile and a thin pair of see- through underpants met them.

A smile found its way to David's lips that told Benjamin everything would work out. But Benjamin hoped that the night would be filled with hot men and even hotter surprises. As the couple found their way through the crowds of naked bodies, Benjamin quickly found himself taken back by the number of men and women being pleasured by one another.

However, seeing the joy that filled each face told the guys that they were in for a wild night. And while making their way through the house of naked flesh, the couple began to overcome the fear that had once been alive in their souls as they entered the house. As they made their way through, they saw couples dressed in leather, with chains and dog collars of different shapes and sizes.

Although neither had seen such before, David found himself becoming intrigued by what he saw. Benjamin, on the other hand, seemed just a little turned off by the usage of leather and chains. However, they could not deny the sounds of pleasure that filled the rooms. The real shock came when a strange yet sexy young man approached David from behind; taking him into his arms and making his body come to life.

Although David disliked the fact that he didn't even know the guys name the way he made him feel took all the resistance away. Benjamin, who had been watching from across the room could feel the anger build inside as he watched the man he loved being pleasured by a stranger. However, that soon changed as Benjamin became a part of the action, and waves of pleasure began to cover the young couple as they watched each other from across the room.

The night ended with David telling Benjamin that they had to find more.

§4 §

The killer found the young man walking out of the party intoxicated with visions of what he had just done.

Although he couldn't decide if he wanted to go home, or to another party, either way, the night had been filled with sexual pleasure. The young man could still feel himself being touched by the hard-bodied man that had just spent the last two hours fucking his brains out.

The party had not been a part of his plans that night, but after reading the ad a few times he talked himself into doing something wild for once. However, once the killer had him in his sights he knew right away that he would kill him. The darkest hour of the night had fallen, as the killer got ready to make his move getting as close as he could before placing the hard blade to his throat. It felt cold as ice next to his skin, but before he could make a sound the blade had done its job, and the blood started to flow like water from the faucet.

The next morning over breakfast David read the story in the paper that took his breath. The headline read young man found dead on the south side. The picture looked just like most young men we pass on the streets every day, but there was something in his eyes that looked familiar. Although it should have served as a warning to the young couple, it didn't. The parties became like a drug to the young couple.

With each one holding a different surprise that the young men had never experienced before, and repeatedly they found themselves being lost in the world that had once never crossed their minds. Three weeks later David and Benjamin were leaving another party when something odd happened. Things had gone well, and once again, the couple found everything they hoped for and then some.

David had tried his first four-way, and Benjamin his first oral experience. Winter had come early that year and the nights had already started to turn cold. That night, with the moon high, the killer found his next victim a slim young man still lost in thoughts of what had happened in the party he had just left. His car was parked down the street so that he wouldn't have to wait for others to move before leaving. The killer had been watching him for over an hour, waiting to see where the night took the young man.

Death would come quickly for this one as the hour was late, and the killer wished to leave before anyone witnessed his crime.

The fourteen-inch blade went in fast cutting the young man across the abdomen as he moved slowly toward his car. Not a sound was made as the killer moved past the young man taking with him another life. The next morning, the papers covered the story without once telling the readers that the victim had been gutted.

Over the next three days, the papers talked about the slain young man, as he remained the cover story. But once everyone discovered the killer wouldn't be found anytime soon the story died taking with it any hope of the public remembering. There were too many unanswered questions and no one to answer them. As the body count continued to grow the city of Richmond started to realize that there was a serial killer on the loose.

§

David had begun to realize that they had lost sight of what they really wanted from the parties, and he told Benjamin that they had to stop or lose each other forever. So, after thinking about all that his lover said, Benjamin agreed that they had to start thinking about a life together, and not the next hot party. The weeks that followed were not easy, but David knew that if he wanted to save what he once shared with Benjamin they had to stop cold turkey, so to speak. About three weeks after their, little wild party days ended, Benjamin decided that they needed to get away, he knew that they had a vacation coming up so he made plans for them to take a cruise for two weeks at the end of spring.

The news of the cruise put David over the top. Just the thought of two weeks alone with the man that he loved, was like a gift from heaven above. David called all of his friends to tell them the wonderful news, and all seemed happy except Sean. Although he said that he was pleased for his friends, David could tell that something wasn't right.

However, when he asked Sean if anything was wrong, Sean quickly said, "No, everything is fine love," "why do you ask"? Nevertheless, David knew he was lying, however instead of fighting with his friend to get the truth, he just said okay, and hung up.

That night David called to tell his family the great news, and everyone was just as happy as he was about the two of them having the time alone. Amanda thought it sounded like a very romantic idea and one that she wouldn't mind sharing with David's father someday.

As the weeks passed David and Benjamin made sure that they had everything worked out for their trip. David had given Sean a key to the house so that he could make sure that everything was safe while they were away. However, just in case he could not keep things up, David's family also had keys.

David and Benjamin had been planning for weeks, and now their big day had arrived. As the two young men said their goodbyes to all of their friends and family David took a few extra moments alone with Sean so that he could thank him for always being such a great friend.

Before David turned to leave, he took Sean into his arms and kissed him goodbye, then turned and walked away. Sean, still floating on a cloud somewhere in space started waving goodbye without really thinking about what he was doing, for he was still lost in the kiss he had just shared with David.

The two lovebirds did not leave their cabin for the first three days because poor David had a bad case of seasickness. However, once the ship came to the first port Benjamin went and found something that would help get David through the rest of the trip without being sick. Once David had a chance to get his stomach back to normal, he found that the rest of the trip was pure pleasure.

Once the ship was on its way again, the two lovebirds were again locked away in their cabin, but this time it really was for pleasure.

Although the trip away was supposed to be about seeing the world, as well as getting their relationship back on track, the lovebirds found themselves lost in passion with no desire to see the world.

Although the trip was two weeks long for David and Benjamin, it seemed to be over just as fast as it began. Still, the couple was happy to have had the time away from the world around them. The trip home seemed longer than when they left home, but even so, Benjamin and David made use of their last hours of freedom.

As the ship docked for the last time, Benjamin took David into his arms and said I wish it could be like this always, just the two of us without the world around us. But even in his dream state, David knew that having the perfect world was just that, a dream.
The drive home was a long one, but one that the guys had been looking forward to for a few days, even though they wanted their trip to go on forever they still missed their home, and family.

David could not believe his eyes as they walked into their home to find that someone had been there doing God knows what. The trash on the floor and the broken furniture told the couple that someone wanted them to be aware that they had been in their home. The sewing table from the eighteenth century was the only piece that made David upset. Not, because it was worth a great deal of money, but because he loved the idea that someone had used it to cloth their family.

Benjamin found a note left for them on their dinner room table that read "*If I can't have you, no one can*"! The letter sent chills down David's back, but he hoped at first that it was a prank left by Sean. However, after looking at the note a few more times David realized that the writing was nothing like Sean's at all. But it wasn't until the police told them about the note being written in blood that David really started freaking out.

The police officer helped them search their home for clues, but sadly nothing had changed other than the note and the broken furniture. David's mind raced back to the wild parties they had been a part of just a short time ago, but he told himself that they had nothing to do with the note or the killings they had read about.

David called his family to ask if any of them had been in the house, but everyone said, no. Within an hour after the guys arrived home, Sean stopped by with their key, but when he walked in, he couldn't believe what he was seeing.

When David saw Sean standing in the doorway, he lost it, and started asking Sean why he did it? However, Sean seemed to have no idea what he was talking about and just looked at David with a blank expression on his face. What would make someone do this David wondered in the back of his mind, but the truth was he had done things lately that he knew were wrong.

And just maybe this was the world's way of saying you know that I know what you have done. The police took Sean into the living room to ask him a few questions, but nothing about the night made much sense to anyone. Officer Bradley Richards seemed lost in thought as Sean began to tell him about the past three weeks. David couldn't help feeling like the world hated him and Benjamin for their past mistakes.

§5 §

Three weeks after the nightmare with the note, all had returned to normal again around their home, but David still wondered why someone would leave such an odd note. Benjamin had been working overtime since their return home trying to make up for the days lost. David had been just as busy working as the flu season had just begun a few weeks after their return.

David had just started to feel safe again when out of nowhere the phone calls started, with someone on the other end telling him that if they could not have him then no one would. David called his parents and asked that they come over until Benjamin arrived home, hoping that by not being alone the calls would stop, but having someone around did very little to stop the Sicko as David called him.

When David's father or mother answered the phone the caller hung-up, but when David answered he would hear the same message as before (if I can't have you, no one can!) the calls had really started to drive him mad. However, he tried to act as though everything was fine so that his parents wouldn't worry about him, or Benjamin. Sara stopped by almost every day after the first night of calls to stay with her brother so that David wouldn't feel so alone, but he always told her and the rest of his family that it wasn't necessary.

Benjamin offered to stop working so many hours, but David would not hear of it because at the time they needed to feel that life was once again normal. Although everyone wanted to understand David's need to feel normal again, they still worried about the young man that wanted the world to believe he was superman.

After weeks of calls and hang-ups, everything stopped just as quickly as it began. David was overcome with joy, but at the same time he could not help but wonder what the Sicko would pull next.

Sean had asked David about going back to the police, but each time David would say" no," because "if we do that then we have to tell them all about our private life and I for one do not wish to share that with any cop." Although everyone understood why David felt a little odd about seeing the cops again, they did feel that he should rethink his stand after the Sicko left them a surprise in the backyard. The dummy hanging from the tree had a note that read (if I can't have you, no one can!).

David called his parents and Sara, but by the time they arrived the Sicko had already made his next move by breaking out their front window while they were in the backyard. Benjamin could not take it anymore and called the police, but when they arrived, they informed the couple that there was very little they could do, except file a report. The officer also informed the pair that they were not the first couple to call them about odd behavior.

Amanda told the guys that they had to come and stay with her and David's father for a few days until they could have someone fix the window and put in a new security system, but Benjamin was less than pleased with the idea, saying that they would be fine in their own home. However, Sara and the rest of David's family didn't seem to care about what Benjamin felt because they had already begun packing David's things, saying that he could come if he liked, but David was leaving that house with or without him!

Benjamin stopped everything to say "look, we don't even know what this guy is after, and to tell the truth I think it's just someone playing a prank, and certainly, nothing that we should leave our home over." However, without missing a beat David's family had his clothes and a few belongings in the car before Benjamin even had time to finish his little speech. Sara then turned to look Benjamin in the eye, and said: "you know what I think; I think you know much more than you're telling any of us because the only one that seems upset around here is David."

The look on Benjamin's face read outrage, but he didn't say a word to anyone just turned and walked away saying "leave if you want too but I'm staying in our home David." David began to cry, asking Benjamin why he wouldn't come with him, what if that sick fucker is waiting to find one of us alone so that he can kill us Benjamin and you want to stay here alone? Please come with me, he begged. Nevertheless, Benjamin walked away saying "goodnight and close the door on your way out."

David knew that he couldn't stay in his house so he left with his family knowing that he would sleep and feel safe with them. The next day Benjamin started calling at eight a.m. asking David when he would be coming home again, but David's father took the phone and said: "he will be home when he gets ready."

David finally returned home after a few days of phone calls from Benjamin telling him that if he loved him then he would come home again where he belonged. The one thing that Benjamin could not deny is that the Sicko had not bothered him since David's departure. That alone started David thinking that maybe the Sicko was after him and not Benjamin at all.

After learning that David was the one the Sicko was after, his parents started talking about hiring a bodyguard for their son. However, David was anything but happy to learn of his parent's idea and he told them at once that he wanted no part of their plan.

Weeks went by without as much as a word from the Sicko, and life for David and Benjamin had truly returned to normal. David had finally started to sleep through the night once again. Nevertheless, Benjamin knew that things could change again if the Sicko made another move. David had been working hard to put his life back together with Benjamin, but still felt like they needed to work on making their home safer.

Benjamin wasn't sure that he understood David's fear of the Sicko, but he did understand that the guy had sent a clear message about his need to control what the couple did with their lives. Maybe, that's why when the Sicko came again he found that the couple had something waiting for him. Although he was not able to leave notes or damage more property this time, he did leave the guys one small gift, he busted their front door to hell causing the alarm to go off letting the world know someone was there again.

When the guys returned home from having dinner with David's family, they found the police at their home along with a carpenter the officers had called to replace their front door. David was once again going out of his mind thinking that somehow the Sicko was watching them from afar, laughing at them as they watched strangers go through every room of their home to make sure that the sick bastard hadn't done even more damage.

Amanda and Sara rushed over to help make sure that everything was okay, and that David was holding up under all the stress, but Benjamin being his usual self-told them that they were not needed. However, that went about as well as telling Dolly Parton not to write songs. Amanda looked at Benjamin, and said, "Young man the best thing that you can do is get out of my sight before I forget that I'm a lady." The leading story on the news that evening was about two young gay men found dead, one with his head cut off and the other stabbed to death. David's family couldn't stand the thought of something happening to David or Benjamin even though Benjamin often showed his contempt for the close bond that David's family shared.

Benjamin's recent behavior was not doing very much to help anyone believe that he truly loved David as much as he said that he did; in fact, Amanda was starting to wonder if he loved David at all. David was not doing very well and by the time the police finished checking the rooms of the house he wanted no part of staying. Amanda quickly started packing his bags telling him that he was moving back home until the sick freak was caught and off the streets.

Benjamin was not happy to find that once again David's family rushed in to take over his life, or at least the life of the man he loved. David was not willing to stay in the house after what had happened, but Benjamin wasn't willing to leave. David tried everything to get Benjamin to understand what seeing their home with its front door gone, and the fact that the Sicko wasn't going away, did to him.

Benjamin thought that everyone was giving the Sicko just a little too much credit for his little games. Once David and his family had left, Benjamin decided that he wanted to go out and have some fun; after all, he had been a good boy just a little too long now. Once he found the perfect club he decided to stay and have a few drinks. However, just as soon as he found a cute little stud the fun began, and the two left for the young man's apartment, where Benjamin would spend the night fucking and sucking his brains out.

Benjamin and his new little friend stayed in bed all weekend. David and his family talked about finding him a new place to live after he and Benjamin sold the house that they're in, hoping that by leaving the house behind they would leave the Sicko behind as well.

When David ran the idea past Benjamin he was less than happy to hear that David wanted to sell their home.

Although he said that he understood that David did not like staying in the house alone, he did not feel that it was a good enough reason to sell their home.

David was upset by Benjamin's lack of understanding about his feelings, but he did try to see things from Benjamin's point of view without judging him too harshly.

After talking to Benjamin a few more times David started to see things his way, after all, maybe he was right about selling their home. Benjamin felt that if they sold their dream home then they let the Sicko win, and to Benjamin that was wrong.
Although David's family wasn't happy about his choice to not only move back into his home but also, not to sell, after thinking about what Benjamin had said about letting the Sicko win.

For David, the Sicko was truly a nightmare come to life, but for Benjamin, he was just a sick individual that had nothing better to do with his time than making others' lives miserable.

Once The Sicko found out that the guy's had a security system installed, he began to ease off. But David couldn't help but wonder how long it would take for him to return with full force. Although things around their home returned to normal, Benjamin was still finding the time to have his fun with the cute young man that he met while David was away at his parent's home. The secrets between the two continued to grow, but David remained clueless.

While David believed that Benjamin was once again working long hours, in truth Benjamin was sleeping around again. Sean had agreed to come and stay with David anytime that Benjamin worked late, hoping that he could help David feel less afraid. Sara and Jason had even stopped by a few times to make sure that David was okay, but each time anyone came by David would tell them that everything was perfect and that they shouldn't worry about him so much.

Although Sara knew that her brother was putting up a brave front, she only asked him two things, "are you really okay? And why not come and stay with Jason and me until Benjamin finishes his new project?" Each time she asked David would always say, "Thanks, sis, but really I am fine, don't worry about me so much."

Benjamin would always arrive home about the same time each night, close to midnight. Not even that, made David feel safe, as he knew that the killer was still out there somewhere. David wondered how long Benjamin would hold up under the strain of working eighteen hours a day, but Benjamin said he was fine even when David knew otherwise.

Benjamin and David hadn't made love in almost three months, but anytime that David tried to talk about it, Benjamin would always say the same old thing, "I'm just a little tired tonight baby, maybe this weekend."

After weeks of hearing the same old lie, David decided that he would catch Benjamin with his pants down, so to speak. Once

Benjamin hadn't arrived home again by seven, David and Sean went out to all of Benjamin's favorite clubs to see if they could find his car, and they did, parked at The Barcode, a really wild club that Benjamin loved because of the young men that frequented the place. Once David and Sean were inside they couldn't find Benjamin anywhere because Benjamin was at his favorite hotel instead. After driving around for hours, David decided to call it a night and look for Benjamin some other time when he felt he could catch him in the act.

That night when Benjamin did arrive home David tried to be as sweet as pie, almost too sweet in fact, Benjamin started to ask what he was up to, when out of nowhere David asked, "are you cheating on me?" Benjamin, stopped dead in his tracks and turned to look David in the eye, and then he said: "No, I am not cheating on you David, and I resent the accusation." "Well, I resent being at home night after night while you supposedly work late," David, replied sounding angry.

"I don't know what to tell you David, other than it's my job, and you knew that when you became my lover, so why is it all the sudden a big problem for you?"

"Your work is not the problem Benjamin, but your cheating is." "I do not know how many times I am going to have to say that I am not cheating on you, believe me, David. And to tell the truth I'm getting just a little sick of you asking me that all the time, he said with a red face that looked like it would explode at any time. David, on the other hand, looked as calm as could be.

Although he wanted to believe that Benjamin was telling him the truth, he still found it odd that he was working late almost every night for months without the extra money, in fact, they seemed to have less money in their account lately.

When David asked Benjamin about the money, he quickly said: "look at what we have had to do in the last few months David, you know that we have had to fix the window, door, and put the system on the house, all of which cost money."

After taking a few moments to think about what Benjamin had just said David started to feel just a little foolish for thinking, that Benjamin was cheating on him once again.

Thankfully, Sean had gone home after he and David returned from looking for Benjamin otherwise he would have heard the couple once again having words over Benjamin's extra sex life. Still, even in the face of defeat, Benjamin continued to claim that he was innocent. David knew in his heart that the man he loved was lying, but he couldn't prove it just yet.

§ 6 §

Benjamin and David had been working hard at putting their relationship back together when unexpectedly the phone calls began again, with the caller saying (if I can't have you, no one can!). David had really started to freak out until he realized the fact that the Sicko only seemed to call when he and Benjamin were doing well together.

The calls would only get worse with time as the voice on the other end became even harder. The messages were filled with threats of abuse and even murder, and David became even more frightened than before.

Once he had time to really think about what the guy was saying he even started to think that maybe the calls were intended for Benjamin in the first place, although, he would have a hard time convincing anyone else; because anytime Benjamin picked up the phone the Sicko would hang-up.

Benjamin even started to believe that David was right about the caller, but even that didn't answer all of their burning questions about why?

It really did seem that the Sicko knew when they were fighting about something because everything would come to a sudden stop.

Amanda and Sara did not share David's feeling about the Sicko, because the guy had already said more than once, in his own way, that he wanted him and not Benjamin. While David wanted to understand why his family felt that way about the Sicko, he really hadn't come out and said anything about which one of the guys he wanted, only that if he couldn't have them then no one would.

Benjamin had once again started working long hours, but this time David could see the extra money in their account at the end of the month. However, all of that changed after the Sicko pulled his next little trick. David and Benjamin had been playing cards with Steve and Johnny, when out of nowhere they heard someone scream, well everyone ran for the front door only to see that someone had set a dummy on fire in their front yard.
Johnny and Benjamin ran out front to put the fire out, while David and Steve called the police.
Although no one was hurt this time, David once again asked Benjamin about selling the house, and as always, Benjamin said that selling the house would be letting the Sicko win.

David had started having the nightmares again, but this time they were about the house burning down with them inside. Benjamin would sit and hold him for hours telling him that everything would be okay if they just held it together a little bit longer because the police would catch this guy sooner or later. Even though David would tell Benjamin that he was right, deep inside he felt like they would never stop the Sicko.

David had come home from work one afternoon three weeks after the fire to find that the Sicko had once again been in their home, and this time he left them a message painted in blood. As he dialed the police, David thought he heard someone in the house with him, but before he had a chance to look, Sean, appeared at the front door. Although David was still a little shaken, he was happy to see a friendly face.

Sean came in and saw the message on the wall, then asked David if he had called Benjamin so that he could come home and be with him? But, David told him that he had called the police instead of Benjamin because he hoped they could find the bastard. However, to tell the truth the police were as taken back by the Sicko as David and Benjamin. When the blood on the wall turned out to be human, David did not like the idea that the Sicko had once again been in their home, not even the high dollar alarm had kept the sick freak out of their home. So, what made Benjamin believe that they were safe?

The officer wasn't able to figure out how the Sicko was able to enter the house without setting off the alarm. Everything seemed to be working as it should, but that didn't help them understand how he got past the system. So, Benjamin decided to call and make sure that the system was still working right, but the company explained that everything was working as it should be, and offered to send someone out the next day to go over the system with a fine tooth comb.

In the meantime, the company changed the entry code to the house, so that no one would know it except, Benjamin and David. And they both agreed to tell no one.

Somehow, three weeks later, the Sicko managed to find out, and this time even Benjamin appeared to be as upset as David himself was. The Sicko had painted a new message across the walls of the living room, telling the young men that one of them was going to die.

Amanda had come just as soon as David called to make sure that her baby was okay, but when she arrived, she found that both guys had bags packed to leave their home. Although she was more than happy to see her baby ready to leave that house, she never thought she would see Benjamin just as willing.

Three days later when the guys returned home they found yet another message on the wall, and this time he cut up their bed. The message read (leave me again and I'll burn the place to the ground because you're mine!) both David and Benjamin read the message repeatedly before they once again called the police. When the officer arrived he took the report and asked them if they believed what the Sicko wrote on the wall? David looked at the officer, and said: "you bet I believe the sick S.O.B. because everything he has told us would happen has happened."

The only thing that Benjamin wanted to know is if the police department was going to keep an eye on their home. However, the officer informed them that while they would watch for any odd behavior near or around their home they could not put an officer on the case full time. Benjamin appeared to be very upset by what the officer said, although it was David that asked the question, "what is it going to take before you protect us, one of us found dead?" The look on the officer's face told the whole story; the police really did not like handling cases that involved gays.

Not three days passed when the guys returned home from having dinner to find that the Sicko had once again paid them a visit, this time his message read (call the police again, and one of you will die!) David looked at Benjamin with a blank look on his face, fearing that if he tried to speak he would start to cry.

Benjamin looked at him and said, "it's okay baby, I feel the same way." They stood there looking at the wall wondering what the Sicko would put them through next. Benjamin called David's parents so that Amanda could once again help take care of her son. It was David's father and sister came to the rescue this time around. Amanda had called to say that she just wasn't up to seeing another message on her baby's wall in blood.

Sara asked if the guys were going to stay even though they knew the Sicko had once again been in their home. Benjamin explained that they had no choice because the Sicko told them that if they left again he would burn the house to the ground. Sara could not believe that someone could be as sick in the head as to try to hurt people without really knowing them. David looked at his sister and said, "we don't know for sure that the Sicko doesn't know us; we only think that he is a stranger, but we don't know that for sure."

Benjamin and David once again found themselves looking at a mess left behind by someone they could only imagine being sick, and beyond help. David had truly hit bottom, the overwhelming feeling of doom had finally set in. Benjamin, on the other hand, seemed withdrawn not really allowing all that had taken place to get to him, as though he thought by pushing the feelings deep down inside it would really make them go away, but he was wrong.

The next few weeks were filled with fixing the mess left behind by the Sicko, but somewhere inside David had found the strength to fight back the fear that lived within.
The fear had become anger, and the anger had started to take over all of his thoughts and feelings, somehow all that once made him a loving and caring young man, turned him mad.

The Sicko struck yet again, this time letting David know that he could see the anger that lived within. Benjamin did all that he could to help David understand that the Sicko only wanted to play games with them because he thought it fun to watch as they fell apart. Everyone wondered if the Sicko had anything to do with the killings.

Helping David see the game that the Sicko was playing took all that Benjamin had left, he had truly used all the strength left inside him to make David feel safe again, but the only question that remained is how long it would last?

David returned to work after being off for two weeks on vacation, but sadly the only thing that he did was fix what had been destroyed by the Sicko. Benjamin used his time off to help fix the man he loved without much success, but nothing would stop him from trying.

David had come to expect the worst anytime they had to leave their home unattended even though they had taken every step available to make sure their home would remain safe. One would think that the Sicko had an inside track on all that the guys did to keep themselves safe from all that he had in store for them, and maybe he did, after all, every step they took he was always one ahead without fail.

However, after weeks of hell the Sicko stopped without warning, David had truly started to believe that the nightmare was over.

In fact, the police had even talked about closing the case for good, when out of nowhere David received a call from the Sicko telling him that he had to leave Benjamin, or watch him die. David was left feeling alone and scared beyond words. However, when he tried to explain everything to Benjamin, he found that the man he loved thought he had lost his mind; after all, the Sicko seemed to always leave his messages in their home, so why not this time?

David could not answer his question because in truth he did not know why the Sicko had changed his plan. After all, no one could understand what made this guy tick.

Benjamin informed David that he would not leave his home because of some message he received from some sick S. O. B., but

David tried to explain that he wouldn't stand by and watch him die because they didn't do what the Sicko wanted. That night after hours of fighting and begging David left his home, and the man he loved to keep them both safe.

Benjamin watched as the man he loved packed all of his belongs into his car and drive away, not knowing if their nightmare with the Sicko would ever truly end.

David arrived at his parent's home that night filled with both rage and hope that the nightmare would end soon. Amanda and Charles greeted their son with open arms, and even though David had a smile on his face, Amanda knew that on the inside her son was dying.

§ 7 §

Weeks passed, and there was no word from the Sicko everyone had started to believe that it was truly over. Then one night about a month later the first call came from the Sicko telling David that he had truly saved Benjamin's life by leaving him. However, David was in no mood to hear anything that the Sicko had to say about what a good job he had done by leaving the man he loved.

Benjamin had really started to believe that he would spend the rest of his life without the man he wanted, and as a result, he had started dating other men. Once David learned of his little dating game, he called on his old friend Cole to help fill his lonely nights the way that Benjamin had started filling his.

Amanda was anything but disappointed to learn that David had started seeing someone without thinking about what he was doing to his chances of making things right between himself and Benjamin once the Sicko was caught.

David did not seem to mind the fact that he and Benjamin were moving further and further apart from one another, without even thinking about the long-term effect it would have on their relationship. Amanda Williams was the only member of the family that smiled when she thought about her son with someone besides Benjamin.

The guys had started playing a game that no one would ever truly win, except the Sicko. Then David started to think about all that his father had said about this being a game to the Sicko, and maybe this was his plan all along to see what would happen if he made them separate. However, the truth of the matter was that the guys hoped that people would believe that they had moved on from one another when in truth, they just wanted people to see them apart.

Benjamin had been calling David every night hoping that he would be able to return home again soon, but after months dealing with the Sicko the guys decided that living apart was too much, and David finally returned home.

They did not leave their home for the three days after, but David, who had always wanted to return home, found sleep hard to come by in his home after the fear that had once died, returned.

David watched as Benjamin slept beside him, and he could not help but remember their lives before the Sicko. Benjamin had always been strong and very forthcoming with his opinion about life and love. However, David had always been just a little shy, never really wanting to make waves for anyone, mainly out of fear of being hated by the people he loved.

Sara had always been such a great help to David telling him that he was free to love as he pleased and that he should never let what other people thought control his life. Although it took time David began to see that, his sister was right about everything, because in the end if we do not love ourselves enough to live the truth, how can we ask someone else to love us.

Benjamin had always been the kind of young man that loved living his life both open and free, so living his life in fear over the thought of some sick bastard that no one had ever met caused the young man to hate what had happened to their lives at the hands of this man. However, Benjamin wanted David to feel safe, so he kept his thoughts to himself.

David had only been home a few days when the Sicko let them know that he was aware of their little reunion; however, his next message would make them wonder if David's coming home had been the best idea after all.

The Sicko told them that they had only one week to decide which one of them would leave their home because if they both tried to stay one of them would die.

Benjamin was anything but happy with the idea of one of them having to once again give up their home, but he always knew that the Sicko wasn't really into games. Knowing that the days would pass with the blink of an eye, Benjamin started trying to figure out how they could beat the Sicko at his own game, but before they had time to come up with a plan the Sicko struck again.

David was about to leave for work when he found what the Sicko had left for them this time; Benjamin 's car had all the windows busted out. David ran back into their home calling Benjamin every step of the way hoping that he had only been dreaming because the thought of the Sicko once again finding his way into their home was more than he could take.

When the police arrived, Benjamin explained that no one had been in the garage that morning until David went to leave for work, and that's when his car was found with all the windows broken out. While the officers worked the scene of the crime, David was on the phone with his work explaining why he would not be in that day. Although Benjamin told him that he would be fine left alone, David refused to take any chances.

David broke down that morning after the police finished their work in the garage, asking Benjamin if he ever thought their lives would return to normal. But sadly Benjamin did not know what to say to a question like that since he didn't know why the Sicko had come after them in the first place, or if he would ever stop. David called his family to let them know what the Sicko had done now, but to his surprise, his mother didn't start bitching about his return home after hearing what happened this time. Amanda was more than happy to help make sure that nothing more happened to her son and his lover, however, even she did not know how to fight someone they had never seen before.

Sara called to make sure there was nothing that she or Jason could do to help, but Benjamin assured her that everything was fine.

As the days passed Benjamin and David grew more aware that, their time together was about to end, and this time it could be for good.

Benjamin told everyone that he would be the one to leave their home this time because David needed to be where he felt safest, and that was in their home.

However, after hearing, what the guys planned Amanda and Charles told them that they could stay in their home for a few days that way they would both be out of the house. David thought his parents had a great idea, but Benjamin, on the other hand, didn't think they would get away with it; after all, the Sicko seemed to find them no matter where they went. Although that was true, David also knew that the Sicko did not know where his parents lived, unless he knew them too.

After thinking about David's plan Benjamin agreed to try it, for a few days anyway but told everyone that the first sign of something going wrong and he would be out.

Amanda and Charles were more than happy to have their son home again even if it was because of a deranged Sicko.

However, something inside David told him that their plan would not last long because somehow the Sicko would find them.

A week had passed when they found the first sign that he knew what they had pulled, but instead of running from the monster, Benjamin decided that they had to face him finally.

Benjamin took David's hand looked him in the eye and said, baby if we don't stop running now we'll always be running just trying to stay one step ahead of the Sicko, and that's no life. Although David understood that what Benjamin said was true, he also had a fear that lived inside about the Sicko not wasting time in killing one of them, and he didn't wish to see that come to pass.

Charles told his son that morning that Benjamin was right about the Sicko, if they didn't take a stand soon they would run out of ways to be together, and he would win.

Well after hours of talking, the decision was made that the guys would return to their own home to fight the Sicko finally face to face.

§ 8 §

Weeks passed without a word from the Sicko, and David had started to feel like something bad was about to take place. Benjamin, on the other hand, thought that maybe the Sicko had given up. Although neither young man could have imagined what was really about to take place because one of them would find himself facing much more than a sick stalker, and the other would be on trial for murder.

The night of the big storm the Sicko made his final move. Benjamin had been working late, or so David thought, but as the night grow closer to midnight he realized that Benjamin had been in their home the whole time watching and waiting. What is this all about Benjamin, David called out hoping that he would be wrong and that Benjamin would indeed still be working, but something inside told him that he wasn't.

Benjamin stepped out of the shadows to face the man he had been with for almost fifteen years now, and the look of shock that covered David's face told the real story of that night. Disbelief and heartbreak had truly found their way into the heart and mind of young David because the man standing before him now was not the man he had wanted to see.

Benjamin moved forward only to fall to the ground; it seemed that someone had shot him. Fear really took over David's thoughts when out of the corner of his eye he saw the figure of a man moving toward him.

David stood there lost in both fear and confusion, wondering what would happen next.
Sean stepped out from the shadows to face the man he had always called his best friend; however, after seeing the look of fear and hate in David's eyes Sean knew that someone would pay for what they had done.

Sean asked David what he thought about his little plan to off him and Benjamin, but David stood there speechless watching the man he had always believed was his best friend pointing a gun at his head.

"Oh my God," were the next words spoken by David as he watched the man he loved dying on the floor. "Why?" Was David's only question, but Sean did not seem ready to answer anything right away? In fact, he just stood there watching Benjamin take his last breath. Once Benjamin was dead, Sean walked over and asked David why he had stayed with that cheating dog for so long.

However, fear had taken David's voice, as he had just watched the man he loved die before his eyes, and there was nothing he could do, but watch helplessly. Sean seemed angry that David failed to respond to his question, so he hit him across the face, with the gun. David fell to the floor only to pull himself up again without thinking about it.

Then he looked Sean in the eye and said because we had something that you never will. "Oh, and what is that", Sean asked? "Love," David said. "Oh, but I do have love," Sean said. "I have your love David, or at least I should. After all, I just did you a very big favor by killing that cheating bastard," he said in a very calm voice.

I have always loved you David, but then again, you have always known about my feelings for you, and yet you still stayed with Benjamin. You have known for years that he cheated on you, and lied to you repeatedly, and still, you stayed with him, "why?"

"Because I loved him", David said. "Sean if that's why you did this, then you made a very big mistake because I won't love you, I'll hate you," David said in a cold voice.

"It does not matter now," Sean said; "because I think, I will let you join Benjamin in hell. However, before I do I have one more question for you?" What is that David asked?" When did you know it was me?"

"I knew when the Sicko only cut up my things, and never Benjamin 's, then there was the way the Sicko talked about what he wanted to do with his love interest it was always his plan to feel me inside him, and never to be inside me."

"Sean I am not as dumb as you believed me to be, and that's why I have already called the police." However, Sean no sooner said "liar!" than he heard the police coming, Sean looked David in the eye and said, "this will never be over." David looked Sean in the face one last time before he made his move.

The police had arrived, but Sean told David to stay away from the doors and windows or he would kill him too. David had always been one step ahead of Sean until now, so without a thought as to what could happen David dove for the gun hoping that he would be able to pull it away from Sean's hand without anyone getting hurt, but that was not to be.

It seemed like time stood still, but really seconds had past when the gun went off killing Sean. David stood there filled with both fear and hate as he looked down at the man he had once called his best friend laying dead on the floor. The cops busted down the front door of his home telling David to drop the gun.

As he stood there looking down at the man he had loved for almost fifteen years, David began to cry. Although he had already dropped the gun before the cops ever busted into his home, David knew that he had taken the life of the man he had once called a friend.

That night the police talked to David until the early hours of morning hoping that they could find a hole in his story somewhere, but to their surprise, his story never changed once.

When Amanda and Charles arrived to take their son home, the look on David's face told his mother that she was in for a few sleepless nights, for anyone that knew David could see that he was in pain over what had taken place just hours before.

However, not even his parents could have seen what would come next.

Three weeks passed, and although David had returned to his normal life, everyone could see that he was still in a lot of pain. Discovering that the man once called his best friend wanted to kill him, and take away the only man he had ever loved, really took its toll on poor David. The only question that remained unanswered for David was if Benjamin had really been involved the way Sean said he was.

The police had found no evidence tying Benjamin to the crime, and in fact, they had found nothing tying Sean to the crime. When the car pulled into the drive of the Williams home that afternoon David knew that his life was about to change forever. The officer knocked on the door and asked that David step out of the house, but before David had time to ask why his mother told him not to say another word until his lawyer arrived.

The next few days were like a bad dream for David, the police had him pegged for a double homicide. The sad truth of the matter was that everything pointed in his direction, Sean had taken great steps to make David look like he was the mastermind behind the whole Sicko game that he and his family had lived through for the last year.

The bigger question for David's family was why Sean had done something so evil to the person he was supposed to love.

David tried to help them understand that Sean had let his need for him take over his heart and soul. Sean knew all about our lives and everything that we had done, and that's what started the wheels turning in his little sick mind, and I guess that's when he started making plans to kill Benjamin and myself.
However, the one thing that he never thought about was my love for Benjamin, although we had our share of problems, Benjamin and I loved one another.

Sean found out that night before he tried to kill me with that gun, but by then it was too late for Benjamin, Sean had already killed him. The days passed like a long dream, and David found himself facing a trial for a crime he did not commit in the first place.

Released on a one hundred thousand dollar bond, David and his lawyer began to build their case.

Alan Thompson had come highly recommended, but for Amanda Williams, he had better be ready to work more than just his good looks and charm. Making sure that David was freed of all charges had become Alan's first of many priorities. Although David had great faith in his lawyer, and his ability to get him freed of all charges, Charles was more than ready to pay any amount necessary to make sure that his son went free.

As David began to share his story with Alan, he could see that Mr. Thompson was happy to hear that he and Benjamin had been together for almost fifteen years. The only hope that David had was to find evidence that could tie Sean to the crime. Working with his lawyer and a detective from the Richmond police force David began to believe that he had a chance of winning the case.

Alan began a search for Cole hoping that by finding him they could help shed some light on what Sean had planned to do with David and Benjamin. However, after weeks of following dead ends, Alan began to lose hope of ever finding Cole. David in the meantime was getting ready to go on trial for murder.

The one thing that both Alan and detective Richards agreed on was hearing David's story about his life with Benjamin and Sean hoping that it would give them some clues as to what he had planned to do once he had David alone. David didn't understand how hearing about his life with the man that wanted him dead, could help save his life, but he was willing to tell his story.

Alan looked him in the eye and said trust me, kid, I know what I'm doing, just tell us all about your life with Benjamin and Sean.

David sat there for a moment thinking about where to begin, then as if someone had whispered in his ear David knew where to start. I first met Sean when we were in our last year of grade school, I was one of those boys that kept to themselves, not because I wasn't popular, but because I liked being alone. Sean, on the other hand, stood out because he was the one of the smart kid with loads of friends. Everyone in school loved him, and every girl in school tried to get him. From the day, we met; I knew right away that we would be friends for life. And up until the other night, that is just what we were.

Benjamin and I met when I wrote an article about school sports for our high school paper, although thinking back now I don't know why anyone would have thought I would do a good job with that one. Nevertheless, I did the job, and after talking to every other team leader, I agreed to meet with a young man named Benjamin Brown to find out more about basketball. Well as you can guess that meeting lasted for many years after the fact. Benjamin had been running late that afternoon, and after almost giving up on him, I found that he not only played the game, but he also coached others in the art of basketball.

Benjamin was very handsome, and well loved by most people, and after spending a little time with him I understood why. His charm was but a small part of a very complex, and well perceived young man. Benjamin knew how to play the game even back then, because not once did anyone suspect that we were lovers.

David went on with his story trying to help them see that even as a young man Benjamin was still a game player. Once we finished high school, I wanted to tell my family about us, but Benjamin told me that coming out would only cause my parent's unnecessary pain and although I didn't understand his reasons for keeping our love a secret I did know that I didn't want to hurt my family.

Although we kept our affair secret from the world around us, people still began to question our relationship. Benjamin would always come up with something odd and off the wall to make the person start to question their own thoughts and idea's making them feel like a fool for ever thinking that something was going on between us, although even to this day I could not tell you why.

At first, I thought maybe he was just a private person, but the longer I knew him the more I could see that his privacy had nothing to do with his not wanting me to tell anyone about us. The real reason behind his little game had a great deal to do with the fact that he was sleeping with other men behind my back.

However, even back then I could not catch him red-handed, so to speak. Benjamin had always been very good at covering his own tracks, but I loved him so I guess you could say that I always looked the other way. Once we were done with college, Benjamin's uncle helped him get his start with Verizon, and I continued to work with Dr. Anderson the man that I still work for today. Benjamin now had a degree in communications, and I had one in nursing. We began our lives together as free adults by telling our families that we were in love.

Although Benjamin's family took the news much better than we had hoped, they still had a hard time accepting the fact that he would never get to be a father. My family, on the other hand, was great they never even said one bad word about our love or the fact that they would never have grandchildren from me.

Mother was the first person to really share in my happiness about finding someone like Benjamin to spend my life with, but I did ask my parents for one last favor. I asked that they never tell Benjamin about our money or the fact that I had a very large trust fund waiting for me when I turned twenty-one. Both of my parents agreed to keep my secret, although they could not understand why I wanted to keep such grand news from Benjamin.

"And why did you?" Mr. Thompson asked. "Why did I what?" David asked. "Why did you keep the trust fund a secret?" "Well to tell the truth back then I told myself it was because Benjamin had grown up in a very modest family, while I, on the other hand, came from a family of wealth, and I did not want to make it seem like I was better than he was."

"Benjamin had always been a very hard worker but when it came to money matters, he was terrible, maybe because, once we had a little money he found it easier to spend it then save it. I must tell you that even though my family had money we learned at an early age that money will come and go, but if you save wisely and spend wisely then you will always come out okay." And with that David said, "Enough, for now, please."

§ 9 §

When David continued his story Mr. Thompson asked that he move ahead to right before they bought the house. Although David does not understand why his lawyer wanted him to skip ahead, he still agreed to do as he wished.

"Benjamin and I had been saving for six years before we bought the house making sure that we had everything needed before we ever started looking. I learned at an early age to pinch pennies from watching my mother, whom before our family had money, used to feed us on one hundred dollars a month."

David became lost in thought not really saying a word just looking off into space like someone that was remembering his life in pieces. Mr. Thompson asked David if everything was okay, but David did not respond right away, in fact, he just sat there looking off as though he had not even heard anyone speak his name. Then without warning, David looked up and said: "that's when it started." The two men looked at David for a moment before asking what he was talking about, but before they had a chance to ask anything David began telling them all about how he met Cole. "Benjamin and I had been fighting for weeks over having a three-way, because I did not like the idea of having a stranger in my home, but Benjamin would not let up until I said yes, because he knew the guy from work or at least, that's what he told me at the time."

"We began making plans once I agreed to have a little wild sex with someone that I had never met. Although in truth I had made plans with my best friend to escape Benjamin's plans, however, Sean stood me up leaving me to face not only my own fears but the truth about the man I loved. Benjamin looked at Cole with a lover's lust, but I told myself that I was wrong about the two of them knowing each other. However, looking back at it now I know that they were lovers and our meeting Cole was part of a plan Benjamin had laid out for me. Hoping to bring me into the world of sex and lies, which he knew I wanted no part of until I got a taste for it myself."

Although anyone that sat in the room with David and the two gentlemen could tell that they were having a hard time understanding what David was talking about.

David started trying to explain what he was telling the gentlemen in more detail, but before he could finish his story, Amanda told them that she had to see David alone.

Although his lawyer needed all the help he could get to help clear David's name, he agreed to a small break so that Amanda could see him alone.

Once the gentlemen left Amanda took her son's hands into her own, and while looking him in the eyes she told him the bad news she had received from the private detective she had looking into his case. "I am truly at a loss for words my son; the detective has only come across evidence pointing to you as the Sicko and not Sean. I have asked that he look deeper into the matter, however, I know that it will only be a matter of time before the police find what he did, and then they will put you back in jail until your trial begins." The look of shock on David's face told Amanda that her son was indeed an innocent man, but the only problem was proving that before the police found anything more against David.

Charles had called in some of the best PI's money could buy to help save his son's life, but without finding Cole, David could lose his freedom.

The funeral for Benjamin had been one of the hardest things David had faced in his life because his one true love was gone, taken away by the man he had always thought of as his friend for life.

The thought of never finding Cole started to take its toll on David, he found himself unable to sleep, eat, or think about anything other than the last words of Sean.

He tried to understand what Sean meant by you will never find him. However, David began to wonder if Cole was still alive, could Sean have killed him too?

So many questions, and no way of knowing the answers, without more help.

David and his family had tried everything to find the missing Cole, but without more time and clues, the odds were stacked against them. Over the next few weeks, everyone working for the family did their best, to make sure that no stone went unturned in the search for Cole. However, David was running out of time, and while he tried to make sure that his parents never saw him cry, David had started crying himself to sleep almost every night.

Sean had done his best to leave no clues as to why he did any of the things he did to hurt David, or anyone else for that matter. Everyone had done his or her very best to keep his spirits up, but the reality of the matter was too heartbreaking for David to face alone.

David had started to relive his life again in his dreams, and at first, he found comfort in them, but now he prayed for them to end. Remembering his life with Benjamin seemed like a bad idea at first, but David hoped that by looking back at their lives together he would come across a lost clue that could help his case.

Amanda and Charles had started to think about what would happen if their son was sent to prison for a crime he didn't commit.

However, Mr. Thompson told them that they had to remain strong for their son no matter what because seeing them filled with fear wouldn't do David any good at this point and time. What Mr. Thompson did not know is that David himself had decided that fighting back was his only hope of staying out of prison. For weeks, David had been living in fear of what could be instead of fighting back.

Although everyone in David's family believed him innocent, David still felt the need to prove it not only to his family but also to the world that he was indeed innocent of any wrongdoing. The body count was now at fifteen, and the police felt that David had done them all.

He knew that the only way to ever find someone like Cole was to go where his kind felt safest, and that was underground. However, just knowing where someone like Cole hung out didn't help anyone find him, for that David himself would have to enter the world of sex and drugs. Mr. Thompson and David's family were anything but pleased with his desire to go into the world that could eat him alive, but David knew it was his only hope.

All his life David had lived the right way and tried to always treat people with respect and kindness, but now that he found himself facing a very uncertain future, he knew that he would have to leave his past at the door in order to have any kind of future.

The one thing that David would never forget were the last words spoken by Sean before he killed Benjamin; without me, you would have never pulled this off, those words had haunted David ever since that night. Even though the police found no evidence linking Benjamin to the crime, David knew that he had been just as guilty as Sean himself had been. Lust had truly taken over Sean's soul, and in the end, it cost him his life.

David had really thought about where Cole could be hiding and the only place that came to mind was the bottom. Although the police did not have the manpower, or desire to check the city over for what could be David's only hope of staying out of prison he did. However, once detective Richards learned of David's plans he agreed to take the trip on the dark side with him. However, what David was unaware of is that his mother offered Mr. Richards a million dollars to help her son. But no amount of money would help her son if the detective found out that he was indeed guilty.

§ 10 §

Bradley Richards would never forgive himself if something were to happen to David, although at first, even the good detective didn't know why. Maybe because he truly believed that David had been framed by his no good best friend Sean, but even that was no reason to risk his life over a guy that he hardly knew. Nevertheless, detective Richards found himself wanting to take care of David, and make sure that he did not go to prison for a crime he did not commit.

The weeks passed like lightning from a storm, quick and steady, but they still had no idea where to find Cole. The only thing they knew for sure is that he never worked for Verizon, as Benjamin said he did. David quickly found himself discovering that the man he thought he knew for the last fifteen years never really showed his true colors at all; in fact, Benjamin had been nothing but a lie. The detective couldn't help but feel sorry for David even though he knew that someone his age should have seen the signs before now.

Even so, Bradley did his best to help David see that none of this was his fault because, in the end, no one made the killer commit the crime of murder. "Going to the parties didn't make you a bad person," Bradley said, "but in truth, it makes you human. Maybe that's why you feel so bad David, but really, there is nothing you could have done to stop any of this in the end," Bradley explained.

Although David understood that he had done nothing wrong, he still wondered if he could have saved Benjamin from himself. David's descent into the world of underground sex took him and detective Richards to Petersburg where they found some of the oddest men they could ever hope to meet.

Bad Boy was one of the first young men that would take the time to answer a few questions about life in the world of hook-ups and raw sex. Although David knew nothing about the underworld of sex and hook-ups he tried his best to do as Bradley had told him before their little journey began. Bradley explained that in order for their little plan to work they would have to make the young men believe that they were looking for some action of their own.

David had changed everything about himself to make sure that no one would ever think he didn't belong, however, Bradley had explained that changing the way he looked really wouldn't make that much of a difference if no one believed them in the first place. Nevertheless, David did as he was instructed only to make everyone think that he was a lover of Bradley's. There were even times when David himself began to believe their little lie, but once he pulled himself together again, reality would bring him back where he needed to be. Just days before their little journey began, David and Bradley had taken the time to make sure that David wouldn't lose sight of what their game plan was, so young detective Bradley explained that in order for the plan to work they needed to talk about a few things.

The look of shock that came over David's face read pure fear. After all, what more would he have to undergo before they could truly start looking for Cole? However, what came next made the young men really think twice about their little plan working out at all.

Bradley explained to David that he needed to see him nude in order for there to be no surprises once their little game with the underworld began. However, it wasn't the shock of hearing about nudity that bothered young David; it was the thought of being with another man besides Benjamin. Then suddenly Bradley began to laugh, asking David if he thought he was asking about sex, because nothing could have been further from the truth, in fact, Bradley had only asked about the nudity because he thought it would help them once they started trying to infuse themselves into the world of which they had never seen the likes.

Bradley was only twenty-five years old at the time but had always been one of the best undercover men his captain had ever seen regardless of his youth. Bradley knew that he wanted to help save David from the prison life because, in the end, most people that enter for killing their lover don't come out without scars.

Their night began with a nice dinner for two, something that Amanda arranged so that the two young men could be alone.

However, as the night came to an end David found himself wanting to know more about the sexy detective sitting across from him, but being shy had always been one of David's biggest hold backs. Thankfully, Bradley could see what was on David's mind, because without a word Bradley walked over and kissed David without speaking. The night quickly turned into an all-out love fest.

David had wanted this ever since he laid eyes on the young detective standing in his living room, even though that night had been one of the hardest in young David's life. Just knowing that Bradley understood what Sean had tried to do, and the fact that he wanted to help clear his name made everything about our young detective seem that much sexier. As the two made their way into the private bedroom, David stopped and took a deep breath as he looked down and saw detective Bradley's penis standing at attention, the size of Bradley's organ made David have second thoughts about being with someone so well endowed. Bradley looked to have about twelve inches of throbbing cock between his legs.

Just the thought of having to share himself with someone besides Benjamin took everything that David had to give. After all, the two had been together for over fifteen years and now David wondered if any part of their lives had been real? Besides, Sean said that he and Benjamin had been planning to kill him for months. Now all he could think about was the task at hand and that was learning to deal with another man sexually.

The night had been like no other for David who had dreamed about sleeping with young Bradley, however, once the two found themselves in bed together everything about it felt natural to both of them. In fact, most people would have sworn the two were lovers for life.

The next morning when the two awoke from the night of passion David was taken back to find that his family had come by to see them off before they left to begin their life in the underworld of sexual pleasure.

As their time with the family came to an end David and Bradley prepared themselves to reenter a world filled with false truths and wild fantasies. The two knew that their time together would be short lived as they only had two weeks left to find Cole, and clear David's name.

Their first night at the parties started out like no other before, but David couldn't help looking around for faces that looked familiar, but only one stood out. The sights and sounds of the party played over in David's memories, not so much, because of what he saw, but because of what he had to do. When Benjamin took him to their first sex party, everyone, one looked normal, like the two of them, here everyone looked wild and just a little crazy.

They had only been asking about Cole for about an hour when out of nowhere a young man wearing a fishnet shirt told them that he could help, but they would have to pay for the info. The look on David's face told Bradley that he would have to step in fast or risk David blowing their cover. The young man explained that money was not something that he found a need for, but a couple of hot guys would work just fine for payment. Bradley asked if Spider, as the young man called himself, had a place they could have a little fun, but he told them that he knew of a great hotel just up the street that would be perfect.

Bradley and David followed him into what David would later call the worst place on earth, but for the night it would have to do. Spider explained that he wanted both of the two studs to have their way with him while he watched them from the mirrors above the bed. And with that said, Spider climbed on the bed and put his legs in the air. Although David wasn't really into having sex at the parties, again Bradley told him that they would have to play the game or go home without Cole.

Bradley quickly took the lead making sure that David had time to see if he could handle what they were about to do. Spider began to cry out just a little as Bradley forced his way into the young man's waiting hole, as David watched from across the room. Thoughts of the life he once had come flooding back to David as he told himself that he had to make this work or lose his chance to find Cole. Bradley played the game well, telling Spider what a great body he had and how much they were going to love fucking the hell out of him.

§11 §

Bradley continued to fuck Spider while David stood frozen watching and asking himself if he would be able to do what must be done to find a killer.

Spider found that having someone as large as Bradley inside you hurt much more than he thought; however, after a few moments of pain he began to enjoy the feel of Bradley.

David stood there watching Bradley fuck the young man silly, but when it was his turn; he wondered if he would be able to make the young man happy.

The thought of fucking a young man he knew nothing about started to turn David off, but he knew that if he didn't give him what he wanted they might never find Cole. Once Bradley pulled his thick hard tool out of Spider, David walked up and entered the young man causing him to take yet another deep breath. Although he had been upset about having to fuck Spider, David soon found that he was more than able to make the young man happy. Once the three climaxed they laid on the bed together for a while just thinking about what they had just experienced together. Although David had been a little put off about fucking Spider, he found that in the end, it wasn't as bad as he had first thought it would be, in fact, he had been very turned on. Bradley was the first of the three to talk asking Spider what he knew about Cole, but sadly, after all, they had just gone through hoping for info. Spider told them very little.

The only clue they now had to work with lead them to another wild party on the same side of Richmond as the last two. By the third day, David had begun to lose hope, but Bradley kept him focused on the job at hand.

Finding Cole would prove to be a much harder job than either of the two men had once thought, but they both knew that without him David was going to prison.

Once Bradley found the next party, he found a hot young man named pretty boy. The young man was willing to talk, but not before the guys agreed to have sex with him and his friend, and they found themselves saying yes without thinking about the outcome. The sex started out rather vanilla like most they had experienced in their lives, but that changed when Pretty Boy started to cry out "hit me, daddy, for I've been a bad boy". David and Bradley had no idea what to think about the young man's odd behavior, but they did what they had to so that he would be willing to talk afterward. The friend seemed unhappy to have to bottom for David and Bradley, but that didn't stop the guys from fucking his ass off. Once they had all gone a few rounds the young man named Pretty Boy agreed to talk. Bradley showed him the only picture that they had of Cole, and right away, he could tell that the young man had seen him before.

However, that didn't stop the young man from lying. And that's just what he did telling the guys that he had never seen Cole in his life, but Bradley wasted no time in letting him know that he knew the truth. After that, the young man started sharing the truth, hoping that he would get another round with the hot detective. But the young man told them that in order to find Cole they would have to meet with a guy named Big D.

Big D hung out at a downtown club called "The Wood". The Wood seemed odd for a hangout, but Bradley had learned that nothing about the world of sex made sense, so you just have to go with the flow of things or find yourself becoming lost.

Big D was the kind of young man that most people feared, not because he was mean, but because he had a very large endowment. David approached the young man filled with fear, but he knew that his only hope of ever finding Cole lied in the hands of people like Big D, and the others from the Parties. Bradley did his best to help David overcome his fear, but inside he was almost shaking himself. Thankfully, for both young men, Big D wasn't in the mood for sex, otherwise, they would have had to add one more name to a list of at least ten other men they had already slept with just to find him. David wanted to make sure that Big D was telling the truth about Cole, but Bradley knew that they had to play it cool, or risk losing Big D's help.

Big D turned the guys onto a yet another young man that he said knew Cole well, but something in David told him that this guy would only lead to a dead end. Thankfully, Bradley did not share his point of view, and he thanked Big D for his help. After two long days of searching, they finally found Bottom Boy the next young man on their list, but once again, they had just missed Cole. David knew that his time was running out fast, but Bradley would always say that the next one could be the right one. As their journey continued David found it harder and harder to resist falling into the lifestyle they had been living for the past week, but he tried his best to remind himself that they were only sleeping with these men to find what he needed to be free.

Bradley had really started to understand how someone could become lost in this world, were sex with strangers didn't seem to bother anyone at the parties. However, David found that a little piece of his soul died with each new man they had to share a part of themselves with, but he also knew that it was his only hope for freedom.

After what seemed like months of trying Bradley finally found where Cole was hiding, however, he didn't want to get David's hopes up until he knew for sure that they would find him this time, after all, every time someone said he was hiding here or there they had always come up empty handed.

That night would end a two-week journey into the world of sex parties, but that didn't mean that Cole could be trusted, to tell the truth about what really happened with Benjamin, after all, he could be a part of the group that was killing all the young gay men?

Cole was anything, but corporative although Bradley knew that making him talk was never going to be an easy job, but he still hoped that the young man would do the right thing in the end.

The night they finally found Cole, David truly believed that his life was about to return to normal, however, nothing could have been further from the truth. Cole would say nothing that would help David; in fact, the only story he told made David look even guiltier of murder.

Bradley questioned Cole for hours that night trying desperately to find a hole in his story, but at last, there was none. Cole would tell the same story repeatedly saying David wished to kill Benjamin, and not the other way around.

Bradley found himself lost in thought when David walked in and asked if he had learned anything useful from Cole. The look of shock told him that Bradley knew no more now than he did before, but David knew that he was telling the truth about Benjamin, but he did not know how to make Cole tell the same story. "Maybe if I offer to pay him money that will help him see the light," David said in a rather cold voice. However, the look on Bradley's face said it was a bad idea.

Later that night, Bradley thought he had found a way to make Cole open up to him, but in order for his plan to work, he and David would have a fake a fight. Although David wasn't sure that Bradley's plan would work, he still agreed to play along. Bradley told David that without him hanging around all the time he could have had some fun while being in the world of hot men, and great sex all week. However, thanks to having someone like him around he never got the chance to fuck any of the hot young studs running around.

David looked at him for a moment before saying another word, then without warning, David stood up and said, "Well how do you know that any of these sexy men would have slept with the likes of you in the first place?"

"Well," Bradley said, "sounds like you may be just a little jealous to me." "I'm not jealous," David said in a rather high pitch voice, "but I don't like being told that I held you back from getting a little ass, when in fact; it was your choice to come with me in the first place."

"Well, that might have been true at the time baby, but now, me and this big tool of mine are about to go out and have some fun without you, and all your problems," Bradley Said.

"No, please, you stay," David said, "I am leaving." Then without another word he walked out of the room, they had shared for the past two weeks. David hoped that their little plan would work, and maybe left alone Bradley could get Cole to tell the truth about what had really happened between himself and Benjamin.

Once David was gone Bradley began his little game of seduction on Cole, at first it seemed that the only way he would make this young man talk was to sleep with him. However, that would soon change when after almost an hour of begging him for the truth Bradley lost his temper and told the young man to talk or I will kill you dead. Cole looked at him for a long moment without saying a word, then just started to cry saying that Sean had planned everything. Once Bradley had a chance to hear his little story, he began to see that there was much more to this story, and without thinking too much about it, he asked Cole whom he was protecting. The look of shock told Bradley that he was truly on to something, although nothing could have made what he was about to hear any easier.

Cole began his story by telling Bradley up front that he would not like what he was about to hear, but nonetheless, it was the truth.

Bradley sat back in his chair and waited for young Cole to begin his little tell of what really happened between himself and Sean. Although as his story began it had very little to do with Benjamin, but it had a great deal to do with David. We met months ago when out of nowhere this guy asked if I would like to have a little three-way fun with him and his lover. Well, to tell the truth, I had never really been into the whole multiple lovers' thing, but the guy was hot so I thought what the hell, it could be fun, so after thinking it over for a few days I said why not. Bradley stepped in; asking which one of the two invited him over for the sex, David or Benjamin? Cole didn't miss a beat when he looked up and said,

David. The look of shock that covered Bradley's face must have shown because Cole stopped his story to ask if he was okay, but Bradley just asked that he keep telling his story.

Well after that first night with the two hotties I knew that I liked what they had to offer and that was great sex, they really knew how to make you feel good.

After a few more hook-ups they stopped asking me over, and when I tried to find out why I was met with the same old line, maybe some other time. Well, I'm here to tell you once you put me down a couple of times I'm done with you no matter how good the sex may be.

"Stop! Right there," Bradley said with a very cold tone to his voice, "how did you meet David in the first place?" Oh, didn't I tell you, Cole asked? We met when I came into the clinic where he works for a physical for a job I had just started working as a dancer downtown. The owner of the place liked to make sure that we were clean of drugs and stuff, you know how it is. Yes, Bradley said, I know how it is, but that still doesn't explain why David would ask you over to sleep with himself and Benjamin.

"Well we just started talking that day about things we had always wanted to try, but never had the nerve so to speak, that's when he told that he and his lover had always wanted to have another guy sleep with them." "So after talking to him for a while I thought maybe it would be fun, so I said why not me, and the rest, as they say, is history." Bradley stood there looking at Cole for what seemed like hours before he said another word. Although something inside told Bradley that Cole had just told the biggest load of crap he had ever heard, he also knew that he had to be sure before he called him out on anything. After all, he could be telling the truth, and that wasn't out of the question. But after spending a little time with David, Bradley found it hard to see him as the wild child Cole said he was. But after being around sick people for a few years on the job, Bradley had learned to never judge a book by its cover.

§ 12 §

Bradley knew that he had to get the truth out of Cole, but the question was how to go about it, without giving himself away.

Bradley also knew that he needed time to really pull himself together, before trying to work the truth out of Cole, after all, what if half of what he had just said was true, and David really did mastermind the whole murder.

Although Bradley had started to have strong feelings for David, he knew that in the end, he would have to do his job, no matter what the outcome.

The one question that always remained stuck in Bradley's head was what David would have to gain from killing Benjamin; after all, he was the one with all the money, not Benjamin. Benjamin, on the other hand, stood to gain millions upon David's death, and Bradley found that to be a wonderful motive for murder. Well, that and the fact that Benjamin loved to sleep around. However, that still didn't tell him anything that he needed to know in order to clear David's name.

Cole, it seemed had found a way that could help them both forget about the entire world around them if only for an hour, or so. However, Bradley didn't find his little plan all that appealing, until he started to think about what they had just gone through in the parties, after that he knew that having sex with Cole could work in helping him get to the truth about both David and Benjamin.

Cole found his way into the room where Bradley awaited with his clothes off, and in bed ready for a wild ride. The two wasted no time in getting down to business; in fact, they had the bed rocking in under five minutes. Bradley placed himself behind Cole, and the well-known wild child found himself unable to take all that Bradley had to offer. Bradley being the kind sweet man he was did not, try and force his way into Cole even though the young man ordered him to more than once, saying that it would only hurt for a moment. However, after a few more attempts Bradley slid into Cole the wild child moaned with pleasure as Bradley worked his way in and out of his tight little hole, hoping that his plan would work. But to his disappointment Cole refused to talk about the case once their little sex act was over.

Bradley, feeling like a failure decided that it was time to see someone that could give him the answers he needed. However, finding David alone wasn't going to be easy, but Bradley knew that it had to be done. David was anything but helpful at first, but once he understood why he had to tell Bradley everything, he opened up. The story he shared that day would haunt Bradley for years to come.

David sat back in the big chair in his mother's den with a tall glass of wine and a fresh pack of smokes, not because he liked smoking, but because after everything that had gone wrong it was one of the few things that helped him relax. David began his story by saying "look Bradley you have to understand that Benjamin and I loved each other, but somehow we allowed ourselves to become lost." It all began about a month after we bought the house.

Benjamin and I wanted to share our good fortune with our friends and family so we decided to have a little party so that everyone could see the house at the same time. Well everything went as planned and the party was a big success, but once our families had gone our friends started talking about things that were going on in their lives. However, no one talked about the good stuff until everyone had been drinking for a while."

"Erik and Brian were the first to bring up sex; however, once they did everyone started sharing. Benjamin and I couldn't believe the things that our friends were telling us, but then again, we did live a rather boring life. It seemed that most of our friends had learned about a little secret group that hosted parties for special people that liked to have that little something extra with their sex. You know, like having more than one partner at a time kind of thing," David said. "But Benjamin and I were not sure that we would be cool with having a stranger in our sex life, but once I had time to think about all the times I knew that Benjamin had cheated on me, I began to wonder if just maybe this couldn't save what we had left of our relationship."

"Getting Benjamin to agree was not as easy as you might think, as it seemed he was all up to sleeping around as long as I knew nothing about it. However, once the stories started, that changed very quickly. Erik told us all about the time he and Brian went to Petersburg for a little party hosted by a couple of lawyers. Erik said, that as they walked in you could hear people's moans of pleasure, and see that there were people in groups of three, four, and even five, having sex together like it was normal as could be.

He told us all about the hot young men at the parties, and what he saw them doing. I for one couldn't believe that people felt that free in front of others, but once you walk on the wild side you understand that it's all about the joy of great sex. The rooms of the party were filled with tan and tone young men all willing to do anything you liked, all you had to do was ask, Erik said.

You would find upon a second look that the young men had more than just great bodies; they also had wonderful toys just for your pleasure. Such as dildo's both large and small. And poppers for those who needed them. They also had paddles for the bad boys and cock-rings for that something extra. Yes, one could say the parties had everything.

And one could also find excitement in the many rooms of the house, each one filled with different kinds of pleasure and pain. Some with swings, others with mats, and you could even find torture racks. Yes, and some of the rooms even had dog kennels filled with hot young men, all willing to serve your needs.

Although I had never been one to think about wild acts of sex with nameless strangers I found myself becoming lost in the world of pleasure and freedom."

Well, that's when Benjamin started asking questions like " did any of them have big thick dicks?" or " did you see anyone taking more than one guy at a time?" but before he could ask anything more I told him to stop because Erik was trying to explain what happened. As he continued his story, everyone gathered around so that we could all hear about the action he witnessed. He said, "there were plenty of young studs there and yes, some of them were very well endowed, but most of the guys were only into having one guy at a time fucking them or at least that's what we thought until he entered a dark room at the other end of the house.

And that's where he found all the really wild men hanging out. And before you ask Benjamin, yes, there were guys taking two and three guys on at a time, and some of them even took more than one guy up the ass at a time. But to tell the truth everyone seemed to be having a great time, as the only sounds coming from the room were sounds of pleasure and not pain. However, after having a look around that night Brian and I decided that we weren't ready to have that much fun all at once, so we left with trying anything."

Missy and Roberta started sharing their story next telling us all about the first party they attended. Missy said they heard about the party from a friend that she worked with. She said that the party sounded hot so after talking it over the two young women decided to try it. But before David could continue Bradley stopped him, by asking what any of this had to do with how Benjamin ended up dead?

David looked at him for a moment before answering his question, and then, he said, "Well if you'll let me continue my story I'm getting to that". So, without another word David proceeded to share his story with Bradley who looked as though someone had just beaten him with a deadly weapon. "As Missy continued her story, everyone started wondering if she and Roberta looked around like Erik and Brian or if they dealt with the problem directly and had some fun? Missy said that as they walked in, the house was filled with candles burning in every room, and the sound of women being pleasured followed right behind. She said that they walked into the first room to see what everyone was doing, only to find there were three women having sex in that room."

"Seeing the young girls breast heave with pleasure made them want to strip immediately, but Roberta wanted to see more."

"Roberta took over telling their story by giving us a full description of the next room filled with young ladies of all shapes and sizes. Roberta said that she watched as one of the couples started to play. The tall thin blond bent down to kiss the redhead's breast, then she started to play with them using her tongue, she would let it flicker across her nipple like a little flame dancing across the room. Then she said that the blond started letting her hand travel down the young girl's torso to her G-spot. The look of pleasure that filled the young girl's face was priceless, Roberta said. But still I wanted to see more she explained, so I stood there hoping that the two young lesbians would really start to get down to business, but that never happened. Instead, they just fingered each other until they reached climax."

"But just seeing how much pleasure, they found in each other's company made me want to find someone to try everything with before that night ended. But, Missy being the particle one said, that there would be other nights and that we had to leave before someone talked us into something we weren't ready for so without a word to anyone we left feeling hot as ever."

§ 13 §

"I Must tell you after everyone left that night I was ready to fuck Benjamin's brains out, just hearing their stories had me as hard as a rock, and ready to fuck all night long. However, Benjamin once again said he wasn't ready for us to sleep together again. I had truly lost all hope of us ever getting things back on the right track, when out of nowhere Benjamin ask me about us attending one of the sex parties, and without taking a moment to think I said, yes. "

"Benjamin knew more about finding wild people than I did so I left it to him to find someone hosting a party. And after about a week he had found just what we were looking for. A couple was hosting a party out in Pawhatan, and that wasn't too far from our home, so we both agreed to try it. That night would change things for us in ways we could have never imagined."

"The couple hosting the party wasn't very hot, but most of their guests were everything the doctor ordered and more. As we walked in, I could smell the sex in the air and hear the moans of pleasure coming from every room. Benjamin and I made our way through the house looking around to see if anyone stood out above the others. But to tell the truth, everyone was pretty hot; however, when I entered the last room I saw the perfect young man standing alone in the corner waiting for someone to take him.

And after looking around for a few more moments that's just what I did. I walked over and started kissing him, his long dark brown hair and chestnut eyes, seemed to sparkle by the light of the candles that filled the rooms. As I made my way down to his crotch I found the real treasure. That young man had one of the biggest dicks I had ever seen, it must have been eleven inches long, and beer can thick.

The look of shock on Bradley's face told David that he should explain what he meant by calling the young man's dick a treasure before Bradley decided he had lost his mind. Well, I guess I should say that the young man's dick was only a treasure if you're into really large tools, so to speak Bradley," David said. "You see Benjamin had what I would call a nice dick, but this young man had that something extra every queen hopes to find at least once in her lifetime. Still, he could see that Bradley didn't understand why someone having a big dick would make you happy, so David decided to move on with his story without another word about the stranger's anatomy."

Bradley stopped him again before he even had a chance to get started, asking him once more why someone would want to sleep with a man that had a dick that big between his legs. Well, David said, "I guess it's because some people really like guys with large tools while others prefer normal men." "And which is true for you Bradley asked?" David looked at him for a moment before he answered, then he said: "I guess you could say that I like them somewhere in the middle." "So you didn't sleep with that stranger that night," Bradley asked. No," David said, "I did not sleep with that young man, I only sucked him off I didn't sleep with him." Well from all that you're telling me it sounds as though everyone was having a great time at these sex parties, so what went so wrong that someone ended up dead?

"Well, I am getting to that" David said," but first I need to tell you what happened next at that party". "Okay," Bradley said, "but I really don't understand what any of this has to do with Benjamin's death or any of the murders for that matter." "Well you will," David said, just sit back a listen and you will understand soon." "Once I had finished with my young stranger I looked up to see that Benjamin had been standing in the doorway watching the whole time, without saying a word.

Once I realized he had been watching me, it seemed to make the whole thing seem just a little wilder somehow. But as I watched Benjamin make his way through the rooms of the house looking for someone that would be exciting to him, I realized that I had just made a very big mistake, because Benjamin was the kind of man that wouldn't just stop after having a little fun he would want to try them all. Well after walking around for what seemed like hours, Benjamin found a young man that would fit into his little idea of a good time. And as I stood by watching the two began to kiss. Benjamin looked as though he might swallow the young man's head whole, but he stopped kissing him and started playing with his chest. I watched as he slowly undressed the young man revealing a tan and tone body of a twenty-something. I could tell right away that Benjamin was turned on by the young man's body and his looks as well. And I have to say that the young man was very attractive, to say the least."

"But as I watched my lover slowly work his way down to the young man's thickly padded underwear I could tell from the bulge that he was going to have a big dick that Benjamin would love, and I was right."

"As Benjamin removed the young man's underpants I watched as he took him all the way to his scrotum, the young man moaned with pleasure as Benjamin worked his way up and down the shaft of his thick penis. Although watching it at the time seemed to take all that I had, looking back now it's a wonder I didn't kill Benjamin myself then and there."

"Well after what felt like hours Benjamin leaned himself over a chair and the young stranger walked around and entered him. The look of shock that filled Benjamin's face told me that the young man was even bigger than I thought. However, after a few more strokes the young man had Benjamin begging for more. I stood there watching my lover getting his brains fucked out by someone that I had never seen before, and there was nothing I could do but think about how much I hated myself for agreeing to come to the party in the first place."

"Once Benjamin and the young stranger finished their little fuck fest, I told Benjamin that I was ready to leave with or without him. And I left alone because as I said before, Benjamin was the kind of guy that wouldn't stop until he had tried everyone at least once. I know that sounds like he was just a sick horny freak, but really Benjamin was a nice guy, just a little wild about sex that's all. Although I'm sure that, you're going to think I'm crazy for saying this, but it's okay because I know better. But watching Benjamin get fucked by the stranger really made me hot in a way that I can't put into words; it was just knowing that he was being pleasured by someone with me in the room made something come over me."

"No," Bradley said, "that doesn't sound as bad as you might think. However, I don't understand why you left Benjamin alone in a house filled with young studs all willing to do anything he wished?" "I don't know why," David said, "but I couldn't stand by and watch anymore, that's all."

"So far, you've told me all about the sex that took place at all these parties, but you still haven't told me how they lead to Benjamin's death." "Well," David said, "I guess the real trouble began about three months after Benjamin and I started attending the parties. I had really started to dislike having sex with people that I didn't even know, but Benjamin was still having the time of his life. He had fucked and been fucked by almost every man that attended the party circuit. But still he wanted more; in fact, he had even started seeing some of his favorite's full time behind my back, or so he thought, but I knew what he was doing the whole time. You see the one thing that Benjamin didn't count on was that people on the circuit talk to one another even when you don't think they do."

"What he didn't know is that I was doing the same. I had met Andrew about a month after Benjamin and I started attending the parties. Andrew was just a few years younger than I was, but that young man could go for hours without stopping. He had long brown hair and big blue eyes, with a tan that covered his whole body, not like the rest of us that only tan on the places that show.

Andrew's gift for fucking kept me coming back for more. I always loved the fact that he smelled of Romance by Ralph Lauren; it was always one of my favorite colognes for men.

Benjamin would only wear it on special occasions when I asked him too. The look on Bradley's face told David that he wasn't happy about what he was hearing, although David understood that his story would lead you to believe that he and Benjamin hated each other, nothing could have been further from the truth. Although David would agree that they had their share of problems, the two had never once thought about calling it quits for anyone.

Bradley asked David if he and Benjamin still found the time to have sex together with all their sleeping around, and although David seemed a little put off by the question he answered by saying, "at least three times a week."

The look of shock that covered Bradley's face told David that he found what he said a little hard to believe; after all, he had just told him that both he and Benjamin had other lovers on the side, so how did they find the time to sleep together? "Well," David said, "I guess you could say that while we both agreed to never really talk about what we did apart from one another, we always found our way into each other's arms at the end of the day, just like anyone else with a secret lover."

"After months of playing the field so to speak, Benjamin and I both agreed it was time that we grew up. Therefore, we decided to stop sleeping around. We even decided to get away for a few days alone, but once we returned home things started to change almost from day one. The day that we arrived home Benjamin and I found that someone had broken into our home and left us a little message that read (If I can't have you, then no one can!) I wanted to believe that it was just some sick joke, but we soon found that it wasn't.

However, Benjamin said that we shouldn't call the police because if we did they would start asking all kinds of questions about our past. And to tell the truth I didn't want anyone to know about what we had done. Besides that, my parents would have died if they ever found out that I had been a part of some wild sex parties. You have to understand that my parents have hosted parties for presidents and congressmen; so finding out that their only son was involved in something they would never understand would have killed my mother."

"I know what you're thinking," David said, as he looked over at Bradley who looked to be thinking something along the lines of what a fool David had been for not telling the police right away. However, Bradley didn't say at all what David thought he would; in fact, Bradley said that he completely understood their reasons for not telling the police.

"Really," David said, with a look of shock on his face, "yes really," Bradley said, with a smile. "I know that if I had been in your shoes, I wouldn't have wanted my parents to know anything about what I had done either."

"Look," David said, "I know that Benjamin and I did some really foolish things, but no one should have to die because they sleep around a little more than they should."

§ 14 §

That night after talking for what seemed like hours, Bradley and David called it a night. David feeling like someone had lifted a very large weight off his shoulders fell asleep right away. But Bradley walked the floor for a while thinking about all that he had learned that night about the man he was supposed to help protect. However, the one thing that kept crossing his mind is why someone would want to hurt someone over not having sex with them anymore.

Bradley was sure that there had to be more to the Sicko than David was letting on, and he was going to find out why.
The next morning Bradley awoke to find himself alone, David had once again disappeared into thin air. Although Bradley knew that he hadn't gone far, he still didn't like the fact that the only man accused of murdering his lover and several others was out wandering the streets alone. The thing that really bothered Bradley

had more to do with the fact that he himself had started to fall in love with David against his better judgment. Although finding yourself falling in love with someone as sexy as David wasn't hard to do, and the fact that the young man had been one of the best lovers Bradley had ever had was the tip of the iceberg. Bradley was very much aware that you should never take your work to bed, but in this case, that seemed to be the only way to get a straight answer out of anyone.

The hours passed quickly, and still, there was no word from David. But Bradley found himself getting more upset than angry. Although he knew that David was just a little wild, he also knew that someone out there could want to see him dead. Besides that, he had really started to care about David, so he knew that he had to find him alone because if word got out that he was missing that would mean a one-way ticket back inside with no way out. But just when Bradley was about to start his search for the missing David, he walked in the front door of Bradley's home with a smile on his lips that Bradley really wanted to knock off, but he held it together until he could find out where David had disappeared to. However, David could tell right away that Bradley was anything but happy about his little disappearing act, so he started explaining why he had left without a word.

"I was out looking for Cole", David said with a slightly shaky voice. "But I'm sorry to say that someone got to him first", David said. "They found his body this morning in the James River; someone had stabbed him in the back of his head, piercing the brain". "What do you mean someone stabbed him in the head?"

Bradley asked, with a shocked look on his face. "Just what I said", David replied. "The police aren't saying much about how long they think he's been dead, but from what I could find out it hasn't been long because a few of the guys I know watched him go into a hotel a couple days ago with someone matching your description". "What are you talking about?" Bradley asked, sounding just a little cold "I'm saying that he was seen with you two days ago, so that means that someone killed him within the last forty-eight hours". "Maybe the same person killed Benjamin?"

"Are you sure that the police found Cole dead?" "Yes," David said, sounding just a little upset over the question. But before he had a chance to say anything, more Bradley started asking him about the last time he saw Cole. David explained to Bradley that he hadn't seen Cole since they saw him together a couple of weeks ago.

Bradley could tell right away that David was telling the truth; because anytime he lied, his voice would shake just a little. Okay, Bradley said we now know that someone out there is killing off people that traveled in your circle of friends. Now we just have to figure out why?" Well, I wish I knew" David said, "but to tell the truth I don't have a clue as to why someone would want to kill Benjamin or anyone that we befriended. Maybe all of this really does have something to do with someone wanting to hurt the people I care about," David said. "But the real question is why?"

After talking for what felt like hours that night Bradley and David said their goodnights, and made their way off to bed, hoping that the morning light would help them find some of the missing pieces to the puzzle.

Bradley awoke that morning to find himself alone; it seemed that David had left sometime in the night without a word. The anger built in Bradley like a tidal wave, but the one question remained, why would David leave the one place he knew that he would be safe from whoever wanted to see him dead? Although Bradley would have to wait almost forty-eight hours for the answer; however, he began his search immediately.

David had left to see the only person that he knew would tell the truth about what was happening to the people in his life, and that was Brandon. Brandon was one of the party boys from days gone by, but he still knew all about what happened on the streets. But in this case, Brandon was just as lost as the rest of the world. "You must know something," David said, with the sound of fear in his voice. "I know nothing," Brandon said, in a rather cold unfeeling manner. But David wasn't just going to give up, so he started asking about the others from the party world. "Look," David said, "have you heard about anyone else dying at the hands of this Sicko freak?" "NO", Brandon said, "but I will tell you this boy, no one is safe that knows you." "What do you mean?" David begged, but it was too late Brandon had closed the door and wouldn't answer any more questions.

Feeling like a loser David decided to go and see the only person on earth that ever really loved him, his mother Amanda. Although Amanda wanted to help her son, the truth was she had no idea where to begin. After all, she had made sure that Bradley worked the case without the knowledge of anyone on the police force.

Making sure that her only son stayed as far away from the prison as possible became Amanda's only goal in life, and paying Bradley a cool million was nothing for a family as powerful as the Williams family. Bradley knew that he had to make sure that Amanda knew nothing about David's disappearance. But what he didn't know is that's where David always ran when he found himself in trouble. Amanda had always been David's strength, and she had always made sure that the world knew what a wonderful son he was.

David arrived back at the safe house on the evening of the second day as if nothing bad had ever happened. Once Bradley discovered that he wasn't hurt, he asked him if he had lost his mind. David feeling just a little angry about being asked; told Bradley that where he went had nothing to do with him. Well, Bradley really lost it after hearing the lack of concern in David's voice, and said well if you don't wish to stay alive what the hell are you doing back here?

David stopped everything for a moment, then looked Bradley in the eye and said: "I guess you could say that I came back because of you." "Why me?" Bradley asked. "Maybe because I know that you care about me," David said, "but then again I could be wrong after all, that does seem to be happening a lot lately." The sad part about the whole thing was that David knew just what to say to make Bradley back off because the one thing David didn't need at the time was one more person thinking he was the killer.

Bradley looked David in the eye and said: "no, you're right about the fact that I care about what happens to you; and, if you try anything like that again, you're on your own from that moment forward."

David knew from the look in Bradley's eyes that he meant what he had just said. But something about the way he said it made him wonder if there was more to what he said than he let on. Maybe it's true what they say about falling in love with someone that's in trouble, or maybe David wanted to see something that didn't exist in the first place. Nonetheless, Bradley seemed happy to have him back safe and sound.

But finding the real killer was the most important thing at the time, and not some dream romance between himself and the man that was paid to keep him safe. David found himself unable to sleep that night for thinking about all that had changed in the last few months. First of all, the man he spent the last fifteen years with was dead and someone out there wanted the same fate for him. But the real unanswered question was, why?

Although David knew that he and Benjamin had been just a little careless when they started going to the sex parties, he also knew that Benjamin's death had very little to do with bad behavior. Someone out there wanted to see them pay for whatever reason.

That night as Bradley laid asleep David made his way into his room and slipped under the covers with him. His reasons had nothing to do with sex, but they had a lot to do with being alone. Maybe because it had only been a short time and learning to sleep alone was the hardest part so far. Bradley being a light sleeper looked up and asked David what he thought he was doing. But before he could reply, Bradley told him to leave at once, because sleeping together was never a part of the deal. Feeling like a fool, David made his way back to the guest room and tried once again to fall asleep. But to his surprise, Bradley arrived a short time later and climbed into bed with him. And as they lay there, together David found himself drifting off to dreamland.

§ 15§

The Sicko moved closer to the gentleman walking to his car. He had just left the party of the week. One filled with hot naked bodies, all of which turned him on. Although he had been with more than his share of the hot men at the party, the gentlemen would soon pay the price. The Sicko found watching the young men at play exciting and somewhat of a turn on, but, after what seemed like hours he began to feel the anger rise in his soul.

No one seemed to notice that the Sicko had been watching them, but it didn't matter because he knew what they had done. The party came just when he needed it the most. After all, the week had been filled with long hours at the office, and not enough free time. The invite had come the usual way, by e-mail. The gentleman read the invitation over several times hoping that he understood everything that the party offered. Thankfully, it had everything he had ever dreamed of.

The only hold back for the young man was his young wife. The two had only been married for eight months, but something had been missing and he hoped that trying to live out his fantasy would help with their marriage. He wasn't aware that having wild sex would cost him his life. He marked the calendar so that he wouldn't miss the date of the party, but something told him that nothing would keep him away.

The party seemed to be filled with everything one could hope for and so much more.

As he made his into the first room he found himself become a part of his first three-way.

After that, then he walked around for about an hour more before finding something else that caught his eye. The second floor of the house seemed to be filled with hot men all dressed in leather, and some even had spiked collars around their thick necks like wild animals.

Upon closer examination, the young man found that some of the hot men even had thick leather bands around the cocks and balls causing them to look swollen and slightly discolored. The rooms in the two-story house were filled with sounds of pleasure and pain, but no one seemed to mind the wild action that filled every corner of the place.

The young man left the party around ten that night, but sadly, he would never see his home. As he walked across the street to his car, he started to feel that someone was watching from the shadows of the night. As he walked, he began to wonder about his wife and if she would still be awake when he arrived home, but he hoped that she wouldn't be.

His head was still swimming with excitement after the party, but he tried to keep things together in his head so that no one would ever know his secret. He walked across to his car, but just as he placed the key in the door, he felt the hit to the back of his head.

As he began to regain consciousness he started to look around the dark room, but his eyes couldn't make out much of his surroundings. The room smelled of old cigarettes, and stale air. Even though the walls had been freshly painted and the carpets cleaned, that didn't help the smell of old tobacco.

The young man began to notice that he wasn't alone after all, but the other person in the room had not yet spoken. The silence would not last long as the Sicko made their way over to the young man. Taking his hand and lifting the young, man's face, the killer asked if the party had been worth his life. The young man didn't respond, but instead, he began to cry unable to control his emotions.

He couldn't help think about his wife, but he wasn't sure that he would ever see her again. Fear now filled his body like a hot liquid, but he still tried to hold back the tears that now ran down his face. The Sicko watched this without saying a word. The game had just begun according to the Sicko, but the young man couldn't stop thinking about his life.

After letting the young man think about what was about to happen next, the Sicko walked over and started talking to the young man telling him word for word what was about to happen to him. The fear that lived in the young man now filled his body like a wildfire. The Sicko had told him that he was about to cut him with a sharp knife, and then he was going to burn him.

The young victim started to pray for his soul, but the Sicko told him to keep his mouth shut or he would shut it for him. Thoughts of his wife filled his head as he watched the Sicko play with the knife and torch. He couldn't help wondering which one the Sicko would use first, but before he could ask, the Sicko cut him across the chest. Shrieks of pain came from the young man as the blade made its way across his arms.

Although he was in pain he still prayed for the killer to release him, but deep down he knew that it would never happen. Pain filled his body as he sat there in the old wooden chair that the killer tied him to just an hour before. The Sicko started to burn the young man at random causing him to cry out in pain like a wild animal.

The young man sat there begging God for an end to his pain, but nothing happened until the killer felt that he had outlived his use, and he walked over and took the young man's life by cutting his off genitals. The room fell silent as the killer began to clean everything around them, making sure that the police would have no clues as to his identity.

The police couldn't understand what was really happening in the city of Richmond, but they did know that someone was killing for reasons they could not understand. The more the bodies stacked up the more the people of Richmond wanted answers. No one could understand why the police didn't know more about what made this killer tick, but everyone wanted someone to find the sick bastard soon. The one true thing that people did know is that the killer seemed to only kill young gay men. But everyone started to wonder if that could change, but the police didn't think so.

The killing of the young man should have helped prove that David was innocent, but because he was out on bond, the police still felt that he could have killed the young man. Bradley was the only person besides David's family that knew for sure that he had done nothing wrong. Finding the killer had become a race against all odds, but David and Bradley knew that they couldn't just stop because somewhere out there was the truth. Bradley called his partner and asked if he could check the file for any clue left behind by the killer, but once again nothing.

Mike Reese knew that nothing about the case made sense, but with murder nothing ever does. So far, the police knew that the killer went after young gay men from all over the Richmond and surrounding areas. No one knew if the fact that all the victims had gone to the parties played a part in their deaths, but one thing was known for sure, everyone had just left one before they were killed. And sadly, all of the victims had been cut and tortured in some way before they were finally given a merciful death.

§ 16 §

THE next week the two found themselves running down every clue that came their way. Sadly, nothing seemed to be working out until unexpectedly the Sicko called David. At first, the two men thought someone was playing a very cruel joke, but once David heard the words (*if I can't have you, no one can*) spoken by the Sicko he knew at once it was him. A cold chill ran down his back as he stood there listening to the words being spoken by the person that had changed his life forever.

The message was simple, leave the cop, or watch him die. David knew at once the killer would kill Bradley without thinking twice. The only question that remained unanswered was what to do next. Bradley thought the two should leave his home at once.

However, David did not share his feelings at all. In fact, he thought Bradley's home was the only safe place they could be at the moment. Just the thought of losing someone else that he cared about made David feel terrified and alone. Benjamin had always been such a special part of his life, and now he had to spend the rest of his days without the man he once called his love. Bradley found himself desperate to keep David safe from the Sicko, but the real question remained how did the Sicko know where they were?

David couldn't help but blame himself; after all, he was the one that put them in danger by going to see his mother. The only surprise came when Jason stopped by to see Amanda about Sara's birthday, which was coming up in about two weeks. However, David feared that he wouldn't be free of the Sicko soon enough to see his sister turn thirty-nine.

Learning to live his life on the run wasn't something that David ever thought he could get used too; however, thinking about dying did help just a little. But the one thing that David had never taken the time to think about was Bradley, and what he had to give up in order to save his life. Maybe, Amanda had asked too much of someone so young, after all, Bradley still had his whole life facing him after all this was said and done. While David knew that he had lived a wonderful life so far, and if this really was the end, he had nothing to feel sorry about.

David and Bradley found themselves once again on the run, and Bradley having to play the caring lover. However, this time they stayed at one of the best hotels in town hoping that by staying out in the open the killer would have a harder time finding them. But they were once again wrong. The Sicko seemed to know their every move, sometimes even before they made it, so after leaving three hotels in a row Bradley told David to tell no one about their plans, not even his mother, Amanda.

Although David knew that Bradley was right, he still found himself telling Amanda where they would be just in case something came up with the family, or she found out something that could help. After all, she had used the family money and her powers to keep David free just a little longer by visiting her old friend, Judge Brown. Bradley had come up the idea to use names that had nothing to do with who they really were hoping that this too would keep the Sicko guessing for just a little longer.

The plan worked, the two young men were able to hide out for almost a week before the Sicko found them this time. However, the real question remained, why did he want David in the first place? Bradley called on his old friend from the force hoping that by doing a few background checks he would be able to learn just a little more about the people involved with the case. His plan almost failed when out of nowhere Amanda showed up to ask why he was having the family checked out.

Bradley hoping that he could make Amanda understand what he had done, tried to explain the reason behind the background checks, but sadly she found his reasons lacking and asked that he stop at once before someone got hurt.

Although Bradley understood her reasons for not wanting the family's dirt made public, he also knew that he was running out of time before the Sicko made a move to kill himself or David.

The only thing that made Bradley really want to keep David safe was the feelings he had for him and not the money he was being paid. Amanda knew almost from the beginning that Bradley would fall in love with David or at least that was her plan. Knowing that her son had fallen in love with the wrong man had always made Amanda feel the need to keep him safe. However, with Bradley Amanda knew that her son would not only be safe, he would be loved.

The Williams family had always been a very big deal in Virginia mainly because they had hosted parties for President's and Congressmen, but most of all because they had always been a family with a big heart and deep pockets. Knowing about the family's past helped Bradley better understand why someone would come after David and Benjamin. However, it still didn't tell him why.

Sara and Jason had started talking about having a baby before the nightmare began, but David wasn't even sure if his sister still wanted a baby after all this. Although the one thing that he should have been thinking about was staying alive, moving from hotel to hotel had really taken its toll on the two young men. Nonetheless, Bradley knew that it was necessary to keep David safe and alive.

David, who had grown accustomed to the best that money could buy, hated moving around from one dive to another. The rooms had all started to look the same by now, with the old carpet that hadn't been cleaned in years. And the walls, all in need of a good paint job or just a good cleaning, once you had lived David's life maybe it really was asking too much for him to stay in places that not even his worst enemy would hang out.

Bradley checked them in once again using false names hoping with each passing day he would get closer to finding the man behind the murders. The nights were the hardest on David because the dreams would come, and Bradley would once again do all that he could to make things right for the man he now loved.

Although at the time David had no idea that the man keeping him alive was also the man that loved him, but as time went on Bradley's feelings began to show more and more. But David made it a point to never say a word about what he now knew was the truth about Bradley. After weeks of moving around the couple found themselves running out of places to hide when out of nowhere David gets the call that could bring an end to everything once and for all.

The Sicko wanted to meet with him alone, but Bradley didn't like the idea, so David told the Sicko that they would have to meet in his room later that night, and he agreed.
Bradley feeling helpless tells David that he can't do this alone, but David refuses to call the meeting off hoping that this will end all the hurt of the last few months.

However, the one thought that ran through his mind was really finding the sick bastard behind all this at long last.
Maybe what they say is true David thought if I know who he is then I'll be able to rest at last knowing that his locked away for life.

But Bradley feeling angry about what David was about to do, tells him that he won't let him go through with it alone; however, David tells him that it's the only way to end all the pain.

"How many people does this guy have to kill before it's too many?" David asked feeling angry, himself "I don't know," Bradley said with a shocked look on his face," but I do know that I want you safe."

And that's when it happened at long last David walked over a kissed the man he had been falling in love with for the past few weeks without thinking twice about it.

The look on Bradley's face told the real story because just by looking one could tell that he wanted to ask, what took you so long? Once the kiss ended Bradley pulled away, and said" that's not going to make things better David in fact, it could make them worse,"

Suddenly David felt angered by Bradley's words, not because he didn't understand, but because after all that the two young men had been through he didn't know why Bradley had to once again pretend like his feelings weren't real. Then suddenly as though he could read David's mind Bradley says, "I'm not saying that I don't have feelings for you David, I'm only saying that it's not the best time to make those feelings known to the world." "Well, I'm not asking you to," David said, without missing a beat, "I'm only asking you to admit to yourself and me that we are much more than just two guys trying to find a killer together."

"Well, it seems to me that you already know that so why do you feel the need for me to say it out loud?" Bradley asked.

"Maybe because it's the right thing to do, have you ever thought about that detective Bradley?"

"Okay," Bradley said," it's true I do have very strong feelings for you David, but right now, my only concern is keeping you alive."

"Look, I understand", David said, "but sometimes there are no second chances, and if you spend your whole life waiting for the right moment, you just might run out of time."

Bradley stood there for a moment lost in thought then he walked over and once again kissed David.

And as the two men made their way over to the bed, David couldn't help but think back to the early days of this nightmare when he and Bradley found themselves lost in the world of sex forced to play lovers so that they could find someone to help clear his name. Now looking back David wondered if anyone would ever know just how much he had lost because someone he called the Sicko decided he needed to pay for whatever he had done that they didn't like. But the thing that hurt the most was the loss of Benjamin to the nameless, faceless stranger known only as the Sicko.

Bradley awoke first and spent the next few moments watching the man he had fallen in love with, sleep. But he couldn't help but wonder if tonight really would end the nightmare once and for all, or was this just another part of the Sicko game? Whatever the outcome Bradley knew that he wanted to make sure that David stayed safe, so he made the call. Once he had Amanda on the line, he told her all about David's plan to meet with the killer and asked that she do her best to talk him out of it.

Amanda was suddenly filled with anger at her only son for even thinking about meeting with the Sicko alone, but she also understood his reasons for wanting the bastard caught.

The time was passing like the wind, and Bradley knew that he would have to leave David alone so that he could hopefully bring an end to the nightmare before anyone else got hurt.

§ 17 §

Time seemed to move extra slow as David and Bradley awaited the 10 o'clock hour. Although neither one was ready to face the unknown stranger, they both wanted the nightmare to end. David sat staring at the four walls that for now kept them safe. While Bradley walked the floors hoping, that time would pass faster so that they would be free to start their lives again. David had started to feel like a crazy man when he decided to find another way to pass the time, by asking Bradley about his life before he became his protector.

Bradley stopped walking once he heard the first question David asked about his past, but from the look on his face, David wasn't sure if he would answer or not. Then without warning, Bradley sat down, and said: "what would you like to know?" "Well," David said, "I was just wondering what you did with your free time before you met me?" Bradley sat there for a moment and then said, "Well I love to play pool and drink a few beers with the guys from work. But most of the time, I like to stay around my home working on things that I can fix for myself, you know like a light switch or something." "What about dating?" David asked. Hoping that Bradley would say that he didn't have the time, but that's not what happened at all. Bradley looked at him for a moment and said: "do you really want to know about the men I dated before you?"

"Yes," David said feeling just a little off about asking in the first place. "Well," Bradley said, "I found the time to date at least one or twice a week, sometimes more, but on average about twice a week."

"I took some of them to dinner, while others I just took straight to bed, oh no pun intended." "None taken," David said, feeling all the blood rush to his face. "And did anyone you work with know that you're gay?" "Uh, yes," Bradley said.

"Most of the people I work with are cool; in fact, some of them have even tried to fix me up a few times. But to tell the truth, they make much better cops than they do matchmakers." David understood what Bradley meant since he himself had lived through the whole, I know the perfect guy for you thing with his friends when he first came out. Thankfully, he met Benjamin around that time, and his dating days were over before they ever really started.

"What about girls?" David asked. "Have you ever dated any girls or women?" "No," Bradley said, "how about you?" "No, David said, I have never even thought about going out with a woman before, maybe because I knew when I was just a little boy, that I liked other little boys. I'm not sure how I knew, but I did nonetheless." "What about you, when did you know that you were gay?" Bradley didn't answer right away; he just sat there thinking over the question David had just asked before he answered. Then he said, "I guess I was about fourteen when I knew that something was different about me, but I was about nineteen when I learned that it was called, being gay."

"And when did you tell your family?" David asked? "Well I didn't" Bradley replied, "my parents died when I was just a boy, and after that, I spent the rest of my childhood in foster care." "Oh, now that must have been a really sad childhood," David said. But Bradley quickly explained that nothing could have been further from the truth because his life as a young man had been pretty good if he did say so himself. "I know that you hear all the bad stories about foster care, but trust me I had great foster parents that really loved me."

"In fact, my foster father was a cop, and he helped me get started when I was young. What about you he asked, when did you tell your family?" "Oh," David said, "I guess I was about twenty-three when I told them." "Why did you wait so long?" Bradley asked. "I guess because I didn't want to hurt them, but the truth was they were better about my being gay than they were about my falling in love with Benjamin."

"You see, mother never did think Benjamin was the right man for me, and trust me when I say she made it a point to never let me forget it. Benjamin had always worked very hard to win my parents over, but no matter what he did, my mother never changed her mind about what a bum she thought he was. My father, on the other hand, did like Benjamin, but he didn't think we were right for one another."

"Sara had been the only one in my family to ever give Benjamin a chance, but at times even, she didn't like his ways. Although I could see their point sometimes, I still knew deep down that I loved him, and that nothing would ever change that." "Well it sounds like to me Benjamin was a very lucky man," Bradley said. "Thanks," David said, "but I think we were both lucky to have found love at such an early age."

"So have you ever been in a long-term relationship before?" David asked, Feeling just a little odd about asking such personal questions, but before he had a chance to apologize, Bradley answered "no." "Although I have dated a few guys" "So you have never been in love before?" David asked.

"Well, I didn't say that" Bradley replied. "I have been in love before, but I'm not sure that he felt the same way about me; in fact, I know that he didn't, because if he had we would still be together now."

"So I guess you could say that I'm the only man that has ever said I love you that you knew was speaking the truth?" "No", Bradley said, "but you are the first man that I felt the same way about". "So, do you think that this nightmare will ever be over", David asked? "Yes, it will end soon," Bradley said, "and then we can live the rest of our lives happy and free".
"Well that sounds good to me," David said, with a smile.

"Don't worry?" Bradley said, "I'll keep you safe no matter what". Sitting there, David couldn't help but think about what he had lived through in the past few months. Benjamin had been murdered and yet no one had a clue as to the killer, and now that same killer wanted to meet face to face.

§ 18 §

Just two nights before the big meeting the killer had found the last victim, a young blonde with sexy blue eyes. His tan complexion made him the killer's dream. Just the fact that he was alone and without the rest of the world, made the killer's heart skip a beat. What told him that he was the one is the fact that the man he hated had spent at least three nights fucking his brains out.

The killer watched as he walked to his car unaware that he was watching him from afar. Or that he had wanted to take him for weeks but waited until the time was right, and now the time had finally come. He moved forward without making a sound, and as he did the young man paid no attention to the stranger moving in like a dark shadow.

Then out of nowhere, he felt the knife in his side, and he heard the voice say "don't move or you're dead". Fear took over the young man's body, as he wanted to hear what the voice wanted next, but nothing was said again. The next thing the young man remembered is coming too in a freezing cold room filled with nothing more than an old box spring covered with rust. But that didn't matter right now, but what did is why someone would bring him here? Could he have angered someone from work, or maybe it was just his friends playing a joke? Either way, he had to call out hoping that a friendly face would show itself, but that didn't happen. When the door finally opened the man standing before him wasn't familiar at all.

The killer spoke telling the young man that everything would be over soon and that he shouldn't worry his pretty little head. Hearing someone speak those words didn't help the young man overcome the fear that now filled his body causing him to shake without control. In fact, the young man's teeth had even begun to chatter due to his nerves.

Maybe this made the killer happy to see that just being in the room caused the young man to nearly pee his pants. Hearing the voice talking to him didn't help much, but the young man did his best not to let his fear show. Although nothing he did stopped the killer from seeing the fact that he was not holding up very well.

The killer made his way over to the young man telling him that he would be free soon. The young man wanted to believe that he would still be alive at the end of this nightmare. But something inside told him that he wouldn't be because this guy wasn't talking about him being alive only free. At first, he hoped that the free part was just the killer's way of saying alive, but after being in the same room with him he knew better.

The killer told the young victim that he was about to hurt him because he couldn't keep his big dick in his pants. "But that's not really why I'm going to kill you," he said, in a voice that read anger all the way. "I'm going to kill you because you slept with him for no reason." The young man asked what he was talking about, but the killer never stopped to answer the question. He moved forward cutting the young man across the face. The scream of fear rose out of the young man from deep within. And this made the killer smile.

He knew that killing the young man would be exciting and worth the wait after all. The young man began to beg for his life asking that the killer allow him to leave without further injury. The killer hit him across the face telling him that he need not ask that question again because it would never happen. The young man closed his eyes as the pain filled his body. But that didn't stop the killer from playing with him even more. He took the blade of his knife and ran it over the young man's body, watching the fear build in his eyes.

Never had the young man been this scared of anything or anyone. But that was changing now. Fear now filled him from head to toe. Nothing made sense now, but that wasn't the worst part of this nightmare. The killer could almost read his mind, and with that, he began to use this ability to cause the young man more pain than he had ever known.

The room was dark except for the one nightlight that was on the far left wall away from the young man. But it still gave off enough light that he could see the killer moving around the room. The room appeared to be empty except for the old rusty box spring, the young man, and the killer. Fear started to take over the young man's body causing him to shake beyond control. The killer seemed to like the fact that he was driving the young man crazy.

Nothing seemed to slow this guy down except when the young man begged for his life. That's the only time the killer gave the young man a break from being cut or tortured. So far, he had been cut all over his arms and torso. And with each cut came the same cries of pain that the killer loved to hear. Then the killer did the unthinkable, and he tied the young man to the old box spring. Fear was now taking over the young man's body like cancer.

Then the killer began to use a small torch to burn the young man's body really causing him to cry out in pure pain. The killer really seemed to love hearing the pain rise in his voice like that of a singer that had just hit the high note in a song. You could now smell the fear coming from the young man as he waited to see what the killer would do to him next. Although he hoped without hope that he would be set free. Something inside told the young man that he would never see the light of day again. Sadly, he was right. After six hours of cruel games, the killer finally took the young man's life.

The killer had burned the young man from head to toe after he had already cut him with his old hunting knife. But really none of that mattered because the final act had been the cruelest of them all. The killer burned the young man's crotch, burning his genitals off. And before that, the killer cut the young man's large dick off even with his hair. The cry of pain that came from him made the killer smile like nothing before. Once his last victim had passed, the killer began to clean the small apartment from top to bottom, making sure that he missed nothing.

§ 19§

David had started shaking just a little more at the thought of having to meet with the person that killed his lover. Although he did his best to help him calm down, Bradley knew that nothing would give David peace of mind until the killer was behind bars. "Come on David," he said, "tell me more about your family."

"What would you like to know?" David asked, "Well, how did they make their fortune, would be a good place to start." "My father had always been a great businessman, and my mother had always been great with people, so they decided to start their own company each of their gifts just helped turn it into a major success."

"Sara and I had always been well taken care of by our nannies, but I must say that we did sometimes miss having our parents around." "So what you're saying is that while your parents shared a home with you and your sister they didn't spend a great deal of time with you?" Bradley asked. "No, I guess you could say that we saw our parents, just not every day. Mother always made it a point to take Fridays off so that we could spend the day together, but our father never took any time away from the company. Charles always said that it was for our future that he worked so hard, but the truth was he worked that hard because he loved it."

"As our family fortune started to grow, my parents started to travel and see the world through the eyes of my sister and me. Although I must tell you that some of the places my parents chose to visit didn't impress me much, but Sara seemed to enjoy them more than I did. Then again, she had always loved the same things as our father."

"Mother and I had always shared a very close bond, which most people wouldn't understand. Looking back now, I wonder if I had taken the time to really try to understand our father if maybe we could have been close too." "Well you cannot go back, but you can change the future," Bradley said. "I know that if I had a chance to meet my parents today, I wouldn't waste time thinking about what I missed out on when I could be thinking about what I had just gained."

With time passing by David found himself thinking more and more about what he would do when it was time to face the killer. Although thinking about the killer made him want to hang on to

Bradley even more, he knew that facing him alone was something that he had to do no matter what.

Bradley walked over and started kissing David as though he could read his mind." I'm telling you here and now that everything will work out fine, all you have to do is trust me," Bradley said in a very calm voice. "I know that in my heart," David said, "but I wish someone would tell it to my head because something up there thinks this will all end in a nightmare."

Once Bradley had David calmed down once again he started telling him about joining the police force, "I remember the way I felt the day I walked in to fill out my application," Bradley said. "I was shaking from head to toe with pure fear. Although my foster father was standing beside me with pride and joy, that really didn't change the fact that I was a gay man wanting to join the force. But once I made it, everyone treated me with kindness and respect. And that's something that everyone should have," Bradley said, "but let's face it, not everyone finds that in his or her job or life."

"About a year after I joined the force, I was placed with a guy by the name of Mike Reese. Mike was a cop's, cop if you know what I mean. He did everything by the book, but you always knew that he had your back, no matter what."

"That was something that I missed once Mike left the force because my next two partners didn't have the same love for the law that Mike and I shared. Therefore, after a short time together I requested a new partner. Although I had started to receive a bad rap from some of the guys on the force, I didn't care because doing my job was the most important thing in the world to me." David didn't say anything for a moment; he just sat there looking at Bradley. Then he said," Well I think that you're a wonderful officer and I care for you more than you will ever know." David couldn't believe the words that had just come out of his mouth, but for some reason, he didn't mind as much as one would think.

Maybe because the fear that lived inside had started to make him see that there were no promises of a tomorrow. Bradley didn't respond at first to what David had just said, but when he did, David began to sob. "I know now that I would die if something happened to you David," Bradley said in a rather sweet voice that David hadn't heard before. "But the truth is I care too much about you now to walk away when I know deep down that I should because I'm too close to the case at hand. But none of that matters now, because I love you." And without thinking about it David said the words, "I love you too."

Their time together was running out as the hour of ten was drawing near. But before Bradley took his exit, he wanted to make sure that they had everything worked out.

§20§

THE hour of ten p.m. was drawing near, and Bradley was getting ready to leave the man he had come to care for alone. But before he left, he took David into his arms and told him how he felt after spending the last few months with him finding a killer. Deep inside he wanted to say the F-word (Forever), but he couldn't bring himself to say it aloud for fear that David wouldn't feel the same.

But David pulled away saying "I know what you mean, and I feel the same way about you, but once this is all over we can really talk about our future. Okay? Now get out of here, so I can meet a killer." Bradley walked away and left the room without a word, knowing that he may never see the man he loved again. Walking down the long hallway Bradley looked around hoping that he would see someone that looked out of place, but no one did.

The time passed as if someone had turned all the clocks of the world to extra slow, but for David, everything was moving in fast forward.

But the knock on the door told him that the Sicko had arrived. As he opened the door, the man standing on the other side astounded David. Sara was the next thing that passed from David's lips. The look of shock that covered his face told Sara that she had been right all along. So we meet again, Sara said in a rather cold and creepy voice, like someone out of the old horror movies, that she and David use to watch together.

"Why are you doing this Sara", was all that David could say at the time. "Well, lover it's like this", she said. "You had all that wild sex with nameless strangers, and I knew that my husband wished for the same fate, only he didn't have the balls to say so". "The thing that hurts me most, my dear brother is the fact that my husband was in love with you".

"Why was that David"? As the words come out of Sara, David could feel the anger that lived inside his sister. Sara wasted no time coming at David again. "Did you really think you could get away with fucking every man in town and no one find out?"

"Well brother you were wrong, I found your little black list about two weeks after you started your little fuck fest, and I made them pay". "I knew that I wanted to make you pay too". "So, I took my time by playing little games with you". "But the most fun was making everyone think you had killed Benjamin". "Oh, don't worry brother dear, Benjamin really is dead if that helps with your pain". "You're sick", David said, without thinking about what Sara would do. Then it happened, Sara walked over and struck him across the face, telling him to watch his mouth or the game would end now. "Sara I'm your brother and deep down you love me," David said hoping that his words would reach his sister. But they only seemed to anger Sara as she watched in silence, the man she had loved since childhood.

David was at a loss for words as he stood there hoping that someone would tell him that everything had been a bad dream and that the man he once loved wasn't really dead. But that wasn't going to happen and David now knew that everything had been a lie. "Sara," he said in the calmest voice he could muster, "if you really wanted to hurt me then why kill so many innocent young men?"

"Oh, brother, that's simple; it was more fun driving you crazy and watching you look over your shoulder. Oh, and by the way, I have to say that killing that dumb ass cop was pure pleasure. The poor thing never saw it coming." "No!!" David screamed, but it was too late Sara had already hit him across the head with a butt of the gun knocking him unconscious. Sara stood there for a moment taking in the sight of David lying on the floor like a dead man, and a smile covered her lips that would have sent a chill down anyone's spine.

As David regained consciousness, he could see that Sara was sitting in front of him holding a knife. Once she discovered that David had come to; she walked over and asked if he was ready to meet his maker. David, feeling like the world was about to end, asked once more, "Why are you doing this Sara?" But she wouldn't respond, instead, she just looked at him with cold steel eyes, which appeared to have no feeling behind them. And David began to fear the worst from his sister, but he did his best not to let her see the fear in his eyes.

David began to think back over the last few months, and he began to see what was right in front of him the whole time. The woman, that he once believed a good person and sister, was really the woman that wanted to see him and his friends die. Really, it all made sense now, after all, Sara was never in fear of her brother dying before because she was the one behind the rest of the murders all around Richmond. At the time David wanted to believe that this was all just some sick dream that was about to end, but he knew it wasn't.

After all, Sara could have killed him, and David would never have known that his sister wanted him dead.

But before he had a chance to ask his question Sara walked over and started to fill in the blanks. "First of all", she said, "let me start be saying you have one of the sweetest personalities, and I have enjoyed being your sister all these years, however, it's time to say goodbye". "About a month after I married Jason I discovered that he had a little secret crush on you, and at first, I thought maybe it was just one of those little things that would pass." "Once I found the list of parties near and around our neighborhood, I started looking into my husband's private life, and that's when I found out that you and Benjamin attended these wild parties".

"Even so, I hoped that I was wrong about Jason, but after watching for about a month, I found him coming out arm and arm with a nameless stranger." "The two of them got in Jason's car and started making out as though they were married." "The sight of it made me sick, but I held it back letting no one know that I found out about his sick little sex life".

"However, deciding the perfect way to get rid of you was something that took a little thought, after all; you were my brother." "Nonetheless, I began to put together the idea of framing you for the deaths of every young man that you and Benjamin had sex with at the parties you two frequented over the last few months." "After that, things became clear to me." "Once I started taking lives, I would make sure the world thought you were the killer."

"But I knew that our dear mother would never see you go to prison, so the next part of my plan fell into place easily." "I found a way to let mother know that she could keep her only son safe and free." "After that, the rest was a walk in the park."
"I simply told her about Bradley, a very sexy detective I met after I destroyed your home the first time."

"Although I wasn't sure that you would fall in love with Bradley, I must admit, that it did give me pleasure to know that you were loved before your death." David didn't respond to Sara's cruel words, but he could see that she was hoping that he would.

David said nothing to try to change Sara's mind about killing him, and somehow this really seemed to upset her. Maybe because she thought the man she had just spent the last few months torturing would fall apart like a scared schoolgirl, but that's not what happened at all.

Sara had started to move about the room like someone lost in thought, when David asked, "how long are you going to wait before they ended this little game."

Again, Sara said nothing she just walked around the room thinking.

David knew just what was happening but refused to say a word for fear that he would not only have a gun turned on him but maybe receive a bullet too. The look on David's face became one of fear, and not power, as he continued to watch his sister walk the floor like a lost woman. David knew that his only hope was to keep Sara talking about what a hard time she had getting over Jason's betrayal, but the question was how to go about it without making her angry.

David looked up at Sara and said, "You knew that I loved you when you started this sick game didn't you?" "Yet, you still found a way to make everything okay for yourself". "Not another word", Sara said, "or I'll kill you now".

"No!" David said, sounding like a crazy man. "You cannot kill me, Sara, because I'm your brother and you loved me once." "Well that's over now," she said sounding even colder than before. "You took everything I loved away from me and now you have to pay," Sara said. "Jason was my husband but once he found out that you and Benjamin went to those sick ass parties that's all it took for the man I loved to cross the line." "Now, he's gone to hell with that sick bastard you once lived with".

"Why would you say that it's my fault that Jason cheated on you, Sara?" David asked. "Because it's true!" She said sounding just a little bitter. "Everything that I had planned for the future is now gone just like my dreams of growing old with the man I loved and married, but you know all about that because I took your love too." "And I hope that you understand that I will also have to take Bradley away from you because you need to feel what I have felt since Jason left me for your kind." "Sick all over!" "Yes!" "Sick, all over David, that's what I live with for the rest of my days when I think about the man that I thought I would grow old with." "But you don't ever have to worry about growing old because once I walk out of this room you will be with the man you loved."

Fear found its way into David thoughts again, but he did his best not to let Sara know. "Sara," he said trying to sound calm. "I'm sorry that Jason hurt you, and more than that, I'm sorry if I hurt you in any way." "You have to know that, I love you." "Oh, and why is that? She asked. "Because you're my brother?" "Well, I'm sorry David, but that's not a good enough reason," Sara said. "I'll tell you this much, I won't make you suffer the way I did Jason and the others."

"What do you mean?" he asked, "Let's just say some of the young men prayed for death long before it took them." "Oh, I spent hours making them relive their sins, and when I grow tired of them, I ended things by killing them." "Yes, even your beloved Benjamin." "He thought he was saving your life, when in fact, he was about to meet their fate." "Death came fast for Benjamin, as I knew that there was no kindness left in his heart."

"Watching the look on your face as I walked in tonight was priceless to me." "Sara", David said. "We can work this out without anyone having to die, but you have to give me the gun." Sara didn't say anything at first instead she just looked at David with cold steel eyes that had no feeling left in them.

Sitting in the silence, David found himself thinking about Bradley and wondering if Sara really had taken his life the way, she said. Maybe she was just trying to make him suffer before she made her final move, and if so why lie about killing Bradley when she so freely pointed out that she didn't mind killing anyone. Once again, David tried to get Sara to talk about what she had done to the others, and once again, he found her unwilling to talk about what happened with the last victim of her game. She was willing to talk about Jason once again saying that watching him hang there like a dummy in a store window really made her happy.

"I spent almost seven hours watching him beg for his life, but he knew that begging wouldn't save him after I cut off his manhood." Shock filled David's face as the words spoken by his sister began to set in. But what she said next really took its toll on his nerves. "Once I had cut off his manhood, I burned him in a few places to help even out the pain that now raced through his body like fire". "Yes, it's true that I loved watching him hurt just as much as he hurt me. Besides, he got to leave the pain behind once death took him to the next part of his journey through this life, but I had to stay here and face what the people I loved did to break my heart."

"Sara". David said, "I never meant to break your heart or anyone else's for that matter, but what you're doing is wrong and I think that you know that deep down." "No!" She said, sounding just as angry as before, but this time you could see the fire in her eyes. David knew that if someone didn't show up soon he would die in that little hotel room alone with his sister, and all of her anger.

Although David wanted to understand what his sister had lived through finding out that her husband played for the other side, but that was still no reason to kill more than twenty other gay men so that everyone could pay for his mistakes. After all, Benjamin had never once hurt Sara or anyone in David's family. But that didn't stop his sister from taking his life, and now she was about to do the same to him.

The room fell silent when David heard someone calling his name and he knew at once that it was Bradley. "I thought you said he was dead," David asked. But Sara didn't bother to answer his question. "Are you okay?" Bradley called out. But before David could answer Sara walked over with the gun and said: "don't speak." Feeling the cold barrel against his skin, David sat there not moving an inch, as the man he loved got closer to the room where his sister held him prisoner.

Bradley called out, "are you okay David?" Still, there was no answer. The room where David was being held fell silent as his sister held the gun close to his head making sure that he didn't make a sound for fear of death. Bradley finally burst through the door after calling out a few more times, but when David didn't answer, he forced his way in.

Sara moved like the wind lifting up her gun and pointing it at Bradley. And he did the same as he had his weapon out before be broke in. Sara told him to lower his gun or David would die, but Bradley refused to listen to her orders. "I know that you love your brother Sara, so why not end this thing without anyone else having to die." "Stop talking," she said, as she brought the gun back to David's head.

The room fell silent once again as Sara and Bradley looked at one another from across the room hoping that one or the other would place their weapon on the floor before someone else died. David tried talking to Sara, asking that she let Bradley leave without harm, but she didn't respond. Bradley, on the other hand, asked David to stop asking his sister for his freedom, and start asking for his own.

The look of shock that covered Sara's face told David that their love for one another was working on Sara. So, without thinking twice David told Bradley that he loved him and wanted him to leave before something terrible happened. Bradley wouldn't hear of leaving him behind, but the look on Sara's face had gone from anger to pure sadness. David could see that his plan to make Sara forget about killing him had started to work. But before he had a chance to act, again Sara went after Bradley. The gun went off without warning, and Bradley hit the floor. Sara wasted no time in leaving the room and her brother behind. David ran over to make sure that Bradley was okay, only to find that he hadn't been shot at all.

Bradley had been wearing a bulletproof vest underneath his shirt, but that didn't stop David from making sure that Sara hadn't hurt him. Once they made sure that neither one had been hurt,

Bradley and David began looking for Sara, hoping that she hadn't gone far. But there was no sign of her anywhere in the hotel. In fact, the guy at the front desk never saw her run past. It was like she had become a ghost.

§ 21 §

The next morning the phone in Bradley's room started to ring about seven-thirty. The voice on the other end said they found another victim in an abandoned apartment. The victim had been tied to an old box spring like a wild animal. His skin had been removed and his genitalia had been cut-off. However, the major shock came when the man said the name, Jason Haywood. David heard the name sitting beside Bradley in bed, and started to cry because he knew that the killer was his sister.

Mike Reese asked if Bradley and David could meet him at the apartment so that David could identify the body. Bradley didn't seem very happy about taking David around the other officers, but at the time, he knew that he had no choice, because refusing to go would only make him look guilty. As they arrived David could see the body of the man he once called his brother in law hanging in the middle of a living room with wounds that could never be described by anyone other than the killer themselves as only they would know what they did to the young man hanging before them.

Jason had been cut all over his body and yes; Sara had cut off his dick even with his hair. But that wasn't the worst part of what she had done to the man she had married just a short time ago. No, that came in the form of burns that covered more than ninety percent of his body. Tears ran down David's face as he stood there looking at Jason and wondering what could have made his sister do something so out of character.

When they were growing up Sara had always been the happy child always willing to help those in need and now she was the most wanted killer in Richmond history. Nothing about what happened made sense to anyone working the case, but David understood the rage behind Sara's actions. Jason had hurt her when she found out that he played on David's team, but had married her to keep his little secret. However, when she found out instead of talking to him about it she decided that revenge was the way to go, and that's what she's been doing ever since.

Jason's body was removed from the rusty box spring, and taken to the morgue. The police hoped that the autopsy would give them some clue as to how Jason died.

Bradley told Mike all about Sara being the killer and asked that he help them find her before she left town for good. But David knew that his sister wouldn't leave town until he was dead. A fact that scared the hell out of him, but made him grateful at the same time, because with him still alive, there was hope of his sister living through this nightmare. Bradley offered to take David back to his parent's home so that he could tell them about his sister before the news channels found out and started telling the world.

David knew that he was right about the news, but finding the right words to tell his mother and father about Sara would be the hardest thing that David had ever done. Nothing about the nightmare seemed fair, but David had to stand up and do the right thing by his family before it was too late. The drive over seemed to take hours when in truth it was only about fifteen minutes. David asked Bradley if he would see him again soon, but the look on his face told him that he would be around for a long time to come.

"Look," he said "you know that I love you and I want to make sure that you're safe, but I also want to bring in Sara before she does harm to anyone else", Bradley said. "But I'm going to need your help." "Why me", David asked? "Because you two are close and she trusts you even though she says that she hates you because of Jason." "And why do you think that?" David asked. "Because of something that I heard Sara say to you right before I walked in." "Oh, and what might that be?" David asked sounding just a little lost.

"She said that she had killed because Jason loved you more than her, and she always believed that you two shared something bigger than just sister and brother." "Why, because I'm gay?" "No, I don't think that has anything to do with it, but I do think that I'm right about your sister." "And I hope that you trust me enough to help me get her before it's too late."

"You know that I will do whatever I can to keep Sara safe, but I will not help you kill my sister so don't ask." "I would never do that" Bradley explained, "but I would like to see her get some help." "Okay, you have a deal, but the first sign of you going back on your word and our deal is off." When the car pulled in David was happy to see that his parents were waiting in the drive, but he didn't understand how they knew he was coming home. But the looks on their faces told the story. They knew about his sister and the fact that he was now a free man. Bradley held his hand as they made their way into his family's home, knowing that their lives would never be the same again.

Amanda and Charles looked lost as David tried to help them understand what Sara had discovered about Jason. However, he could see right away that they didn't understand that Jason had been homosexual. "What are you talking about?" His mother asked, sounding a little frustrated over what she was hearing. Bradley told David that he would happy to help, but was met with a no thank you. David went on trying to help his mother understand what he was telling her. But nothing seemed to work until he said look she killed them all.

Charles stood up and said, "your sister couldn't be a killer she is too sweet to be a serial killer." Amanda however, knew that her son was telling the truth after seeing the pain in his eyes. Bradley sat with the family for a short time after making sure that David would be okay to leave alone with his parents. But he could tell right away that they loved one another regardless of what he had once thought about the oddball family.

Sara being a killer would make for wild headlines in all the papers, but with the Williams family's money, they would be able to keep the bad press to a minimum. No one could believe that Sara had turned out to be the killer, but once David told his parents about her holding him at gun point they knew without question that their only daughter needed help.

Amanda asked Bradley if there was a way that they could put Sara into one of those hospitals for sick people so that she wouldn't have to go to prison. But the look on his face told her that they would have to act without help from the police force. "I'll do whatever I have to Mrs. Williams, but your daughter will be going to prison".

Bradley waited until he and David were alone again before he asked. But the time had come and he needed David's help or Sara could end up in the morgue with all of her victims. "We need to find out where the next party is going to be held so that we can set a trap for her." "And what makes you think she's going to kill again", David asked? "Well, let's see," Bradley said, "She's angry at the world because the men that she always thought she could trust have let her down in her mind." "And I'm sorry to say that one of those men is you." David didn't speak for a moment, and then he said, "I know that your right but I want to keep her alive."

Bradley agreed to make sure that Sara stayed safe, but something about setting up his sister didn't set well with David. But then again, nothing about having a killer for a sister made sense. Benjamin had died at her hands and now he knew that Jason had too. But the oddest part of all was knowing that the person he loved more than any other was the person behind the killings. Something about the parties made David's skin crawl as he began to search the Internet for the next hot spot, only to find that there would be six parties that night instead of the one from the old days. Yes, it seemed that the killings had caused the world of gay men to go crazy because they were having parties left and right.

Nothing about any of it made sense to Bradley or David but they knew that they had to find out which of the parties Sara was most likely to attended. David felt that they should focus on the west end of Richmond, but Bradley thought it was too predictable. "Sara will go outside of her comfort zone because she knows that we are on to her."

"Maybe," David said, "but hasn't all the murders taken place in the west end so far?" "Yes, but we both know that the only reason for that is because Sara brought them to the west end." "Okay, but that doesn't mean that she will go to the north or south just because the police know that she is the killer. In fact, I would think that would make her want to hunt close to home,"

Although they didn't agree about Sara, David and Bradley still found a way to look for Sara without driving each other crazy. Bradley went to the south side hoping that he would be the one to find Sara. While David took the west end feeling, that he would find his sister first. And David was right Sara was sitting outside the last party of the night. The party was taking place at Wilde Lake apartments number 214.

Sara was parked across from the building where all the young men were having their fun. David wanted to make sure that no one hurt his only sister, but he always wanted to make sure that Sara didn't hurt someone else. The night was warm and muggy with the moon shining high above, but for Sara Williams Haywood it would be a night of endings.

David walked over to his sister's car and opened the passenger door, and Sara looked at him as though she hadn't seen him in ages. "What are you doing here?" She asked sounding like an innocent child. David told her that he had come to help, but Sara didn't seem to understand. Thankfully, he had called Bradley before he walked over or things could have gotten bad quick.

Sara looked at her brother for a while before she asked again, "Why are you here?" Although David told her that he was there to help, Sara didn't seem to like that answer. Nothing about the night seemed to be going right for anyone, but least of all Bradley who was about forty minutes away. Although he was driving like a crazy man he still hoped that he could get to David and Sara before something bad happened. David refused help from any of the other cops saying that he would tell his sister what was going on if anyone besides Bradley tried to bring her in.

Keeping Sara safe had become this unwanted job for David, even though in truth he wanted to see her pay for what she had done to him and the rest of the world. "Sara", he said and he took her hand "what are you doing sitting out here on such a warm night?" "Nothing," she said, "just watching the young men having their fun that's all. What are you doing here?" She asked once again, but this time with a touch of anger in her voice. "I told you," David said, "I'm here to help you stay safe." "Safe from what she asked?" "Well, from yourself honey, because you're sick." "I'm not sick," she said sounding really angry now.

David took a few moments to think about what to say before he told Sara that she needed to see a special doctor that helped people with their heads. No sooner, had the words left his mouth and Sara had put the knife back to his throat. "I'll kill you dead you little bastard", she said as she held the knife close to the skin causing a thin line of blood to run down the blade. David didn't move even though the knife wound hurt like hell.

"Please let me help you" David begged, but Sara didn't seem to want to hear the cries of help coming from her brother. "I know that you don't want to hurt me Sara, and I don't want to see you hurt either. So why not put the knife down so that we can talk about this without anyone being hurt?" "No", she said as she pushed the knife deeper into David's skin. The blood was now all over David's front as he tried his best to help his sister see that what she was doing would only lead to her death if she didn't stop, but nothing seemed to work.

§ 22 §

Bradley had been driving eighty miles an hour racing against time to get to David and Sara. But the only thought going through his mind was if David would still be alive after all this time. David had taken his heart without much effort and that alone scared the hell out of detective Bradley Richards, but he knew in his heart that this time it was love. Nothing in his past ever felt like this and that's why he had to make sure that his lover survived his crazy sister.

Racing down 288 toward 64west Bradley couldn't help wonder if he had done the right thing letting David go off alone looking for his sister.

But in his heart, he knew that no one would have been able to stop him. David wanted to keep his sister safe from the rest of the force for fear that they would just shoot and ask questions later. Sara needed help and not from some gun crazy cop looking to make a name for himself by killing one of the worst serial killers in Richmond history.

The Williams family had helped many of the local companies over the years, but when word got out about Sara, everyone seemed to forget what the family had done for them in the past, and that didn't set very well with Amanda. In fact, she told her son that once all of this came to an end they would have to make some changes to the family's portfolio.

As David waited with Sara hoping like hell, that Bradley would save him once again. Sara looked like a wild animal seated beside the man that she once loved more than life. David wanted to understand what had turned his sister into a killer, but nothing about what she had done made sense to him. Maybe it was true that Jason had been a gay man that married a woman, but that was no reason the kill so many innocent young men.

The blade of the knife had started to cut deeper bring with it more blood, but David did his best to remain silent. Sara looked like she was about to cry out in pain as David once again tried to get her to understand what was happening to her. Sara, began to cry as David told her that help was on the way, but just when he thought things were about to get better Sara pulled the knife closer to David and said: "don't fucking move."

Nothing about Sara's actions made sense to David who thought he was getting through to his sister only to find that she was still on the verge of killing him once again. Sara looked into the eyes of her brother doing her best to understand what was happening to her and the rest of the world. Nothing about what David said made sense to Sara. Could it be that she didn't understand what she had done? Maybe she could say that she didn't understand what had happened to the young men that had been killed, but David knew that she understood the other night when she told him all about what she had done to Jason.

"Sara," he said, "Why are you doing this?" David asked. Sara didn't answer and instead, she forced the knife into his chest causing blood to run down his body once again. David held back the urge to cry out. Something about feeling the pain surge through his body told David that he wouldn't be able to hold back much longer.

Bradley had been driving for what felt like hours when he found that he only had about five miles to go before he reached his beloved David. Thoughts of what could happen ran through his mind as he found himself thinking about all the bad things that could be happening to David and the rest of the young men that found themselves standing before a crazy woman.

Bradley pulled into the parking lot and he began to search for Sara's car a purple two-door 1979 firebird. Although the car was now a classic Sara had made a few changes that made the car a little more modern. Finding a purple car with a large gold bird painted on the hood shouldn't be too hard, but when you're searching through a parking lot with more than thousand cars it can take a little time. Time that Bradley clearly didn't have. David could feel the fear rising in his soul as he began to see his own life flash before his eyes. Sara was starting to cry again, but David had never stopped trying to help his sister understand what was happening.

Bradley had been driving around the parking lot for about ten minutes when he finally found Sara's car parked just outside the singles. Nothing about the night seemed to make sense, but Bradley did his best to make sure that everyone made it out alive. David spotted Bradley driving near and hoped that he could spot the car parked over in the dark shadows of the night. The clock on Sara's dash read twelve midnight, but he felt like he had been awake for days instead of hours. Sara must have seen the relief in David's eyes because the next thing he knew she was yelling "move and you die."

Bradley moved in once he found Sara parked over in the darkest corner of the parking lot. Before he left the car Bradley called ahead to let the rest of the force know that he had found Sara parked in the parking lot of Wilde Lake Apartments. Bradley exited the car and walked over hoping to find Sara willing to turn herself in, but that wasn't the case. David appeared to be safe, but he could see the blood that had been running down the front of his clothing.

"Are you okay?" Bradley asked. But before he could answer the question David was told to keep his mouth shut. Sara seemed angry about what was happening around her, but David tried to help her see that everything would be okay if she did what Bradley said. However, Sara didn't seem ready to listen to anything that David or Bradley had to say about what she should do, and without a word, Sara started the car.

Bradley couldn't move fast enough and Sara hit him on the side as she drove out of the parking lot heading for Broad Street. Calling ahead letting everyone know that she was heading their way seemed to be the only thing that Bradley could to help David. Everyone said that they could see her car coming their way, but Sara was racing down the street at such speeds no one could see for sure that it was her car.

But everyone knew that she was the only person racing down Broad Street at that hour. Four other officers were racing after Sara each traveling at speeds of one hundred miles per hour. David began to pray for God's help, but Sara told him to stop or she would kill him. Thoughts of what could be, raced through his head as he watched his sister race down Broad Street with four other cars racing after her.

David asked that Sara pullover, but she didn't seem to understand what he said, and if she did she didn't care to listen. Someone from behind them was calling out over a bullhorn for Sara to pull over, but instead, she sped up. Thankfully the streets of Richmond were dead at that hour of the morning or someone would have gotten hurt. Sara was driving at speeds David had never seen before, and yet he prayed the officers would be able to pass her. Sara showed no signs of slowing down, as the race for nowhere seemed to carry on forever.

Bradley was calling David's cell phone but Sara wouldn't let him answer without being hit across the face with the gun she had taken out of her purse about a mile back. The fear had started to show on David's face as he watched his sister heading down a one-way path to hell. Bradley stayed close as the race down Broad went on with everyone doing his or her best to keep up. However, the changes that Sara had made to the old car made keeping up harder than anyone had thought possible.

The officers could not use any of the modern methods to stop Sara, so they would have to depend on their skill. David tried once again to reach his sister who seemed lost to the world after starting this little wild goose chase down Broad Street. Nothing about Sara's behavior made sense to David, but he still did his best to get her to stop the car. However, nothing he said seemed to make that much of a difference to his sister who was driving her car like one of the NASCAR drivers.

Everyone was racing after each other hoping to end this without anyone being killed, but the more time that passed the less likely, it was to come true. Sara seemed to want things to go on forever. Even when the officers moved close she managed to pull ahead once again leaving them wondering if they would ever be able to catch her, something about the way she was driving gave Bradley an idea on how to stop her. Once again, he took the lead asking that the other officers pull back and let him get close to Sara so that he could make sure that David was still alive.

Everyone agreed and once again, Bradley raced against time to save the man he loved. David looked on in silence as the man he loved tried like hell to catch up with his sister's car. Sara seemed to be running on autopilot because nothing anyone said seemed to make any difference in the way she acted. David asked repeatedly for her to pull over and not once did Sara say a word.

Bradley finally managed to catch up long enough to see that David was alive and trying to stop his sister without getting them both killed. His only other choice would be to grab the steering wheel, and that could cause them to lose control and crash. Once Bradley saw that David was still alive, he asked if the state police had managed to get ahead of them from off 64, but no one answered. Fear had started to fill his body as he watched the man he loved being taken away by his sick and deranged sister.

David wanted to believe that everything would end with him being saved by Bradley, but in truth, he would be happy just to come out alive. Sara wasn't showing any signs of slowing down, and the police weren't letting up either. Broad Street had become the raceway for Sara and the police as everyone tried to keep up with one another.

They were coming up on the second Target on Broad, having long since passed the other. Much of the beloved city laid asleep unaware that outside on the streets of Richmond a killer drove like a mad woman.

With the police in tow, Sara and David had passed through red light after red light in Sara's quest to avoid the police. But the question David didn't understand is why she hadn't killed him too? Could it be that she still loved her brother after all that they had lived through together? Or was she just waiting until she felt safe from the police before she made her final move? Either way, things would have to end soon as the race down Broad was about to end. David held on as Sara raced down the street leaving behind several police officers, and the press who had started covering the story about ten minutes after the race began.

The night seemed like a bad dream as the cars continued to race down broad showing no signs of stopping until the deadly end. But just when David thought Sara would stop she pulled a fast one not only on him but the police department too. But by now the state police were involved with trying to stop Sara before she did any more harm. Interstate 64 became the new raceway as Sara made the bold move to leave broad behind.

David started to pray hoping that someone would be able to save him and his sister before something happened that couldn't be fixed. Bradley watched in total fear as the man he loved was being taken away once again by his crazed sister. So, many questions found their way into his head as he raced after the firebird hoping that something would happen soon to end the nightmare. Although it seemed like hours had passed in truth only about thirty minutes had gone by.

Sara still held the gun close at hand ready to kill her brother if need be, but David believed that she wanted him alive or he would already be gone. As the police closed in once again, the bullhorn came blaring through the night telling Sara to end this race before someone got hurt, and once again, she paid them no mind. David jumped at the sound of the familiar voice asking Sara to end this before someone got hurt because it was Bradley. Even at this hour of the morning, David could still manage to think about the people that he would be leaving behind if Sara chose to take his life. But nothing about death really seemed to bother the young man that now found himself a prisoner of his sister's making. Would there ever be a peaceful end to this nightmare or would someone have to die? That question remained at the forefront of David's thoughts as the race down 64 continued.

As the race continued, David began to cry, not so much out of fear, but more out of a need to end this nightmare that had been going on for close to an hour now. Bradley remained hot on the trail of the firebird hoping that this would all end with Sara going to prison or at least a hospital for the mentally insane. The cars raced down 64 breaking record speeds as the police tried to stop Sara without causing harm to David or themselves.

Amanda and Charles waited by the phone for any news about their children while watching the nightmare unfolded before their eyes on T.V. Yes, the news channels were giving the story top billing saying that the city of Richmond was holding its breath while the race to stop a killer continued. No one could believe that Sara had done any of the wild and evil things that the press was saying, but in her heart, Amanda knew that it was all true. Charles stood beside his wife as the T.V. showed their two children racing down Interstate 64 at speeds near 150 MPH. Holding their breath Charles and Amanda Williams watched as the car being driven by their daughter went up in flames.

David realized that something had just happened to the tires causing Sara to lose control just for a moment, and that's when he made his move diving out of the car onto the Interstate without regard to his own life. Bradley watch in total horror as the man he loved fell from the car rolling clear of the roadway, but not without sustaining serious injuries. Moments later David heard a loud popping sound and then his sister's car went up in flames.

The dark night sky became filled with the bright light of the fire as Sara's car went up in flames taking with it a local television station's helicopter, and two state troopers. The flames rose to the heavens taking with them the lives of several people including Sara.

The nightmare was over for most people, but for David Williams and his family, it had only just begun as the press wanted to know everything about Sara and why she chose to kill. Amanda wasted no time in making sure that her family remained private. Having to face the fact that their only daughter had been a serial killer was hard enough without having to face the press every minute of the day.

David had been rushed to St. Mary's with a broken arm and several bumps and bruises and cuts to his chest and throat. Although no one could understand how he survived without major injury, Bradley Richards was just happy that he did. Standing beside David's bed he once again spilled his heart hoping that David would understand the word he was about to say for the second time in his life, the first being two days ago when he told David that he loved him.

Although David wasn't aware of the fact that Bradley had never given his heart so freely before he still understood that he was lucky. Finding love at any age is a blessing and when it comes out of the darkest nightmare of your life then it must be blessed David thought as he laid there listening to the man he loved saying the words that played like music to his ears.

§ 23 §

Three weeks after the nightmare ended, things in David's life still hadn't returned to normal. But that didn't stop him from trying to move forward with his life. Bradley had decided to take some time off so that he could personally take care of David while his body continued to heal. Amanda and Charles had been by their son's side night and day since the nightmare ended, but the loss of their daughter still hit the family hard.

The police had been questioning David for days about what happened in the hour and a half that he spent alone with his sister, but David wouldn't talk telling that he had no memory left of that time. Although no one believed his story, the officers couldn't force the young man to talk.

Bradley wanted to understand why David wouldn't tell anyone about what Sara said in her last moments of life, but he still hoped that he would share anything that could help the police understand why she killed in the first place. Even after David knew about his feelings for him he wouldn't share that part of himself with Bradley or anyone else for that matter. Amanda asked her son if Sara spoke about her or their father, but David wouldn't say. Not because he didn't want to but because he didn't want to hurt their feelings. After all, he knew that Sara hadn't talked about anyone besides her late husband and the men she killed because of him.

Weeks turned into months and everyone began to live their lives again without fear, but the nightmares from that night still played in David's head. Sara was driving like a crazy woman saying that she would never let them take her before her work was done. But not once did she tell David what she was talking about. He asked himself over and over if there was something about his sister's words that could help the police and maybe the world understand what she did. Nothing about that night made sense to anyone that lived through it, but for David, that was truer than anyone would ever know.

Bradley had moved the last of his things in the guest room of David's new home not wishing to move too fast for fear of causing David to change his mind. After selling, the house that he bought with Benjamin David decided to move closer to his parents. So at least he could feel safe again. The dreams had been the hardest part to overcome but slowly he was able to leave them behind too. Mike Reese had been stopping by at least once a week for the past three weeks making sure that David was holding up under all the pressure of the nightmare with his sister and the press.

Bradley couldn't help but feel like he should have done more to keep David safe from the world, but anytime he tried Amanda would step in telling him that she would always watch out for her own child. Things in their lives had truly returned to normal, but before they could truly close the book Sara had to be laid to rest.

Yes, the funeral was long over, but in their hearts, the young woman they all loved still lived on because thinking about her as a killer hurt too much. Amanda and Charles thought about having their only daughter laid to rest outside the state of Virginia when David told them that they would be making a mistake by putting Sara so far away at the family's property in Louisiana.

The press had started to let the family have some peace after weeks of driving them crazy for the next big story about the woman that became the most famous killer in the history of Virginia. Although no one should ever be happy about people remembering you as a killer, for poor Sara Williams Haywood that would be the case forever in history as she had become famous for killing more than twenty people without the help of another person, or so everyone thought.

That was about to change when Mike Reese showed up out of nowhere to visit with David saying that they needed to talk about Sara. David couldn't understand why this guy wouldn't accept the fact that he wasn't going to tell him anything about his sister. Nonetheless, he agreed to talk to Mike hoping that this would be the last time. Mike came into the living room behind David saying "look I know that you don't like talking about Sara, but we need to know what she said that night before you left the car."

David didn't understand the question, but once again, he told the officer that he couldn't help him. Mike seemed to grow just a little angry at David's lack of concern for his need to understand what Sara said before she died. Bradley had gone to pick up a few things in town that morning and David had started to wish that he had gone himself.

Mike continued to ask his questions hoping that David would say something that he could understand. "Why, do you want to know about my sister's last words Mr. Reese?" David asked. "Because I believe she left behind a clue that could help us better understand why she killed." "Well, I'm sorry to tell you once again, but I cannot help you." "You can't or you won't" Mike asked? "Okay, have it your way Mr. Reese, I won't help you."

But I will tell you this much, my sister said that she was never alone." "You know Mr. Williams Sara was right about her never being alone because I was always right there at her side like the perfect lover should be." David cleared his throat hoping that he had just heard the officer wrong, but in his heart, he knew he hadn't.

"Why", crossed his lips before he could stop himself, but Mike was already answering the question before he asked. "It all started when I met Sara one night after she discovered that her husband played on your team. Something like that could really hurt, a woman like Sara, and it did her heart was broken into a million pieces. We started talking that night and she told me all about her need to make the bastard pay, and that's when I told her that I could help." "I knew that would have to make the world think that it was some sick asshole just wanting to rid the world of gays, but in truth, it was a woman wanting to make the world pay for turning her husband into a freak."

"So, you believe that the world should have to pay for the fact that my sister fell in love with the wrong man?" "Well yes", Mike said sounding like a crazy man. "Someone should have to pay for you people being born, but we couldn't just kill mothers without taking out their sick son's first." The words played in David's head like a bad record, and he began to understand that Mike Reese had come to finish what he and Sara began together.
David wanted to cry out, but he knew that it would only make things worse.

Keeping things calm at this point seemed to be his only hope, but Mike must have read his mind because he said: "call out if you want, but no one will hear you." Fear began to rise in David much like it did the night he and Sara raced down Broad Street and the Interstate. The only question now is would he come out of this one alive? Mike took David into his arms and forced a kiss out of him, and David tried to pull away but couldn't. Mike then pulled him by the neck out the door of his home and into his car. David had started praying once he understood that Mike wasn't the nice guy he pretended to be. Once they were driving down the street Mike asked David if he thought his life would end at the hands of his favorite officer, but David wouldn't answer for fear of what would come next.

The car moved down the road like lightning, and fear rose in David like never before. Mike had his gun in his right hand, while he drove the car with his left. Thoughts of what could have been filled David's mind as he wondered if Mike would kill him fast or slow. And the biggest question of all was would anyone know that a cop had taken him away? After all, no one was around the house that day not even his parents. Amanda and Charles had left town two days before hoping that some time away would help them overcome the loss of their daughter.

Bradley would have no idea that his own partner was about to kill his new lover without thinking twice. But David knew that he still had hope as long as he was still alive. The car raced toward the city, but before they reached Richmond Mike took Interstate 295 south. David couldn't help but wonder where they were going, but fear kept him from asking too many questions.

"I know what you're thinking Mr. Williams and yes; you're about to die." But the look on David's face told Mike that he was wrong about David thoughts. "Well let me see if I can help you better understand what's going to happen," Mike said in a cool voice that read I'm in control. "First off, I'm taking you somewhere that I know you will never be found unless I want you to be, and second I'm killing you because Sara didn't get the chance." "Yes, it's true that your sister wanted you to pay just like the others because the problems all started with you."

David didn't understand what Mike was talking about, but he knew that Sara blamed him for Jason being gay even though in truth he had nothing at all to do with her husband's sexuality.

Jason had been this kind sweet young man with a soft voice and kind eyes. Yes, it's true that he was handsome and some would even say sexy, but the fact that he liked both men and women had nothing to do with the kind of person he was or the fact that he loved Sara.

"Oh, so you think that sick bastard loved your sister", Mike asked sounding cold as ever. "Yes, I do," David said doing his best to sound calm. "Just because someone is bisexual, that doesn't mean that they cannot love someone with all their heart male or female." "And you think that this Jason loved both men and women?" "I don't know," David said, "but I would like to think that he loved my sister regardless of the fact that he liked sleeping with men." "Oh, and that makes it all right?"

"No, I didn't say that," David said, "but I will tell you this loving someone is hard work regardless of your sexual preference."

"What you don't understand is that love is a gift and not something that we are owed by the world." "You see Mr. Reese I understand that love is a gift from God, but from the sound of things you and my beloved sister hadn't learned that lesson." "I don't think I should be taking love advice from the likes of you Mr. Williams." "And you would be well advised to keep your mouth shut from now on."

The look of fear showed on David's face as he watched Mike play with the gun that would most likely take his life, but he did his best to hold everything inside as the car raced to his destiny. "Please tell me again why you're going to kill me when you know yourself that if Sara really wanted me dead she could have killed me herself?" "I told you why," Mike said sounding angry at the question. "Sara would have killed you when the time was right, but she wanted to reach our favorite spot first, but Bradley spoiled our plans."

"But this time I made sure that he stayed out of the way until I had finished my work." "And trust me when I say this Mr. Williams you will die today."

Nothing about what was happening made sense to David who had been praying for God's help since they left his home. He knew that Bradley would be back from town by now and realize that he was gone, but would he know that Mike had taken him? After what seemed like hours, the car took the exit for Interstate 64 toward Virginia Beach. "Are you taking me to the beach to kill me?"

"No", Mike said, "But you're getting close."

Fear covered David's face, as he knew that his time was running out. But he still tried to remain calm in the face of death. Mike turned himself in the seat so that he could almost face David who had started to cry without warning. Not because he feared the man now facing him, but because he couldn't control the anger that now filled his body. "I still don't understand why you feel the need to finish something that you said my sister started with you Mr. Reese," David asked.

"Look," Mike said, "I've already told you that Sara and I were friends and she wanted you to die and that's what's about to happen." "I understand that you have fallen in love again with my partner, but he will have to learn to live without you the way that I'm learning to live without my Sara." "Oh, I see," David said, "you loved my sister is that it?" "And if that is true then why would you kill her only brother just because you think that's what she wanted?" "Look", David said, "I knew my sister much better than you did and if she wanted me dead that night I would have been dead." "Sara wasn't the kind of woman that left unfinished business."

"Is that right?" Mike asked.

"Yes," David said, sounding angry.

"As I told you before I knew my sister well."

"But not well, enough to know that she was killing all those young men right under your nose." "Yes, but Sara would have never done such without help from a sick bastard like you", David said. "Watch your ass Mr. Williams or death will find you much sooner than you would like."

David fell silent as he watched the crazy man seated next to him race down the Interstate driving him to his end. David thought that he could talk Mike out of killing him, but so far, nothing he said seemed to make much of a difference. Bradley was David's only hope he thought as the car began to slow down. The exit sign said Williamsburg, and David knew that his time was running out fast.

Bradley had only been back a moment when he discovered that David was gone. The first thought that came to mind was that his parents had returned early, but after looking around, he knew that wasn't the case. David had been feeling under the weather for the past few days, but Bradley knew that it was because he had just gone through hell.

Facing the fact that his sister had become a serial killer, and was responsible for more than twenty people's deaths took a major toll on David.

Bradley looked around the house that he now shared with David hoping that he would find a note or something telling him where he had gone off to, but nothing. Fear began to rise in his soul at the thought of someone hurting the man he loved, but Bradley refused to think about David being in trouble.

The car pulled down a long dirt road that leads to a small subdivision where new construction was all around. David knew at once that Mike was going to kill him and leave his body where no one would ever think to look, under concrete. David knew right away that his fate was sealed. Mike was going to kill him and put him in the ground where they would be pouring concrete in the next day or two. That way no one would ever find his lost body.

Bradley began to panic at the thought of losing David, but then he remembered his cell phone. So, he called his friend at the phone company for help and thankfully, she was able to trace David's phone. When Bradley heard where David was, he knew right away that someone had taken him, and that Sara had a partner after all. The clues had been there the whole time, but no one wanted to believe that two people could be so cruel. Sadly in today's world that is nothing new.

Bradley left at once driving like a crazy man hoping that he wouldn't be too late. David was doing his best to stay calm as

Mike Reese walked around looking for the perfect spot to dump his body. Nothing about what had happened made any sense to David, but he now knew one thing for sure, and that was that his sister hadn't been as crazy as everyone thought.

No, Mike was the real crazy bastard behind most of the killings that had left Richmond reeling in pain that would take years to heal. No one felt safe anymore, but with time that would pass, but for some, the loss would be too much. Lives would be changed forever without anyone taking notice unless it affected them in some small way.

Bradley was driving down 64 west toward 295 hoping with all his heart that he wouldn't be too late to save the man he loved.

Amanda and Charles Williams asked that Bradley do everything in his power to make sure that their only child remained safe, and Bradley was doing just that. He had called ahead asking that the local police check out the location he had on David's phone. The officer told Bradley that it sounded like the new subdivision being built outside of town. The officer sent out two cars to check things out, but Bradley knew that David's life was in serious danger.

Mike Reese walked over and told David that his time had come. David looked at the man standing before him and said: "do what you have to, but I'm not moving one more inch." Mike didn't seem to mind the fact that David wasn't willing to move. In fact, he seemed happy. "Do whatever you wish boy because your time is coming to an end." "Yes, sadly in just a few moments you'll be with your beloved sister in hell."

David couldn't stand looking at Mike so he closed his eyes hoping that it would help him stop shaking like a leaf. The sounds of sirens broke the silence that had befallen David and Mike as they stood out in the middle of nowhere. David had been asking God for his help, and now he knew that his prayer had been answered.

Bradley had once again saved his life, and David knew that he was the one behind the cops showing up out of nowhere. Mike looked shocked to see the cops pull around the corner and the bullhorn saying drop the gun. Although he didn't respond to the order David knew full well, that Mike heard what the officer said. Then out of nowhere, Mike took David by the arm and told the cops to back off or he would kill him where they stood. The officer told Mike to calm down, but David knew that wouldn't help him much. Mike wanted to make sure that Sara's wishes were carried out no matter who he had to kill.

The thought of dying that day didn't seem to bother David as much as knowing that his parents had been through pure hell over the last few weeks and now they could lose him too. The standoff seemed hopeless at first, but once David had a few moments to think about what was happening he realized that all was not lost. Bradley was on his way he would do anything to make sure that David came out of this alive.

Mike watched in disbelief as the officers surrounded them telling him that there was no way out without dying. But even that didn't seem to bother the man that had taken so many lives before without giving thought to those left behind to deal with the pain that would live in their hearts forever. Bradley made the last turn before pulling into the lot where Mike was holding David at gunpoint.

Nothing but hate ran through his body as he watched in fear as Mike held the man he loved, but Bradley held everything together as he began to talk to Mike asking him "why?"
Nothing could shock the officer that had seen everything over the past few weeks including young men hung upside down with his body cut and skinned. No, after that everything else in life seems small. David stood still hoping that someone would able to shoot Mike, but that never happened.

The dance began with the cops telling Mike that there was no way out, and David holding back the tears that wanted to leave his body. Not so much out of fear its self, but a need to feel something. Bradley looked on hoping that this would all end with Mike being killed and not David. Bradley moved about trying to find the perfect shot, but not once did Mike give them the chance to take him out.

No one understood why Mike Reese had crossed the line, but David wanted to believe that things would work out in the end for everyone. Nothing about the day seemed normal to anyone, but Bradley looked on in fear that he would never be able to hold the man he loved again, but David held on to the hope that Mike would change his mind.

"Please Mike; can't we talk about this without anyone else having to die?" David asked. But Mike didn't seem into having the same old talk about setting him free. Fear once again found its way into David's heart and tears began to fall down his face again. Bradley watched wanting to take away the pain but remained helpless like the rest of the officers that stood by watching Mike hold the gun to David's head.

Thoughts of his life with Benjamin filled David's head along with the memories of his childhood in Richmond. Nothing about his life had been easy, but he knew now looking back that he wouldn't change a thing. Mike Reese could take away his life, but he couldn't take away the love that lived in his heart. Bradley called out asking David if he was okay, but Mike wouldn't let him responding saying "answer and you die." David fought back the tears that tried to make their way down his face as the police watch the crazy man holding him hostage.

Everything seemed to move in slow motion as Bradley rushed in to take the gun from the man he once thought of as a brother. Now the only thing that anyone could remember about that moment is that Bradley did the impossible by saving David's life. The next thing anyone knew Mike Reese was heading out back toward the Interstate. The officers took off after Mike hoping to stop him without anyone getting hurt.

They drove at speeds reaching 180 MPH, and still, Mike showed no sign of slowing down. A sense of Deja Vu came over David and Bradley, as they knew full well what was happening out there on the roadways. Mike was driving like a crazy man trying to escape while the officers raced to stop him. Nothing about this made sense to anyone and certainly not those that had just lived through it. Sara had always been a kind and loving young woman and the same could be said about Mike Reese. So, the question remained what would make two people that had never done anything to harm others suddenly become killers?

As the race to stop, Mike took the officers back to the Interstate everyone wondered if this would end with more death or would the Mike give up? Everything seemed to move in slow motion as the officers moved in for the kill so to speak. But not once did Officer Mike Reese slow down. The gunshot seemed to come out of nowhere, but when it hit his rear tire, he lost control and went into a tailspin. The car began to flip before it finally went up in flames. And everyone took a small sigh of relief that no one else had been hurt. And from the looks of things, the nightmare was over.

§ 24 §

Three days after the nightmare ended Bradley and David found themselves once again in the spotlight. Everyone wanted to know what it felt like to be held at gunpoint by an officer of the law, but David wasn't ready to face the world just yet. Bradley did all that he could to stop the pain from taking over David's soul, but sometimes the best thing we can do is let the person we love feel the pain. Amanda warned Bradley that stopping David from dealing with the matter first hand could cause her son to never overcome the loss of his sister and Benjamin.

Weeks passed like a dream, but for David, the nightmares kept the spirits alive. Yes, the spirit of his sister and Mike played with his dreams causing the young man to awake in cold sweats at night. Bradley wanted to once again take away the pain. But at the time nothing would change the fact that David felt like he had caused the death of all those young men. Even though in truth he had nothing to do with their deaths. Guilt had started to eat away at his soul while the rest of the world tried to help him see that he was the lucky one.

Amanda wanted to help her son, but even she couldn't take away the pain that now lived in his heart. Charles offered his only son a trip abroad hoping that the time away could help him come to grips with the fact that nothing that happened had anything to do with him being a gay man or that his sister had lost her fucking mind. Yes, it's true that the family thought Sara had lost her mind in the end over the fact that Jason turned out to be gay, but the real truth was never that simple. Could Mike Reese have turned Sara into a killer, or was it the other way around, no one would ever know for sure?

The shock of a lifetime came when the officer from the state police stopped by to tell the family that no body had been recovered for Mike Reese, and they offered to help protect David, but the family said no thanks. David thought the nightmare was over, but sadly, that wasn't the case. Mike Reese had lived to see another day.

Or at least, that's what David believed even though the officer told them that it wasn't uncommon for a body to be burned beyond ashes when in a fire that burned that hot. It seemed that Mike wasn't just driving around without his share of secrets, and one of them being a trunk filled with explosives. From the look of things,

Mike not only wanted to kill David but himself as well. David wondered if life would ever return to normal again or would he spend the rest of his days living in fear?

Bradley held him tight as the two made their way back into their home. Although no one could say for sure that Mike Reese had burned up in that car, Bradley wanted to believe that the nightmare was over. Amanda told her son that living his life in fear of the unknown was no way to live so David decided that he was going to forget about Mike and Sara.

Life would return to normal as days turned into weeks and weeks into months. Bradley and David grow closer as time went on and everyone seemed happy once again.

David couldn't help but think about all that life had put him through every now and again, but nothing could change the fact that he was happy and in love. Bradley had been wonderful making sure that David remained at the front of his life and that he never took a back seat to anything or anyone. And after a while, David began to believe in happily ever after.

§ 25 §

Months passed and David began to fill safe, but Bradley never wanted to let his guard down. After living the nightmare of a lifetime, Bradley couldn't help but feel like things weren't over just yet. Yes, Sara and Mike were supposed to be dead but in this life, there really are no guarantees.

Mike was killed in the fire or so everyone believed, but Bradley wanted more proof. In fact, he needed it to move forward. Although the family had taken every step possible to make sure that everyone felt safe, Bradley couldn't let the feeling go that something was waiting for them to let their guard down.

Something about living through hell and coming out the other side alive made Bradley and David as close as two people could be without being joined at the hip. David loved the fact that he once again found the man that could steal his lonely heart, but his mother couldn't help but think he had moved too fast with Bradley. Having lived through the nightmare of losing Benjamin and Sara, She thought that her son should take more time to heal.

Charles couldn't help but feel the same way about his only child, but he was on the side of love, understanding that nothing in life worth having was without its risk. David had learned to live life by the seat of his pants and to never think about tomorrow without living today. Making his new house a home had become his new priority in life, but Bradley wondered if David should return to the real world again.

David had talked about returning to work for Dr. Anderson, but so far, everyone was able to talk him out of it. But Bradley knew that it was only a matter of time before the man he loved left the nest for good. Yes, it's true that you can only smother someone for so long before they start to fight back needing their freedom, and with David, that time was coming fast. Amanda and Charles knew that their son had always been strong because that's how they raised their children. Although they neither one thought, they would have a killer for a child. Keeping David safe was important, but not as important as letting him live his own life.

David finally talked everyone into letting him shop by himself after months of babysitting. Mike Reese was long gone David said, as he stood before his parents and Bradley that morning telling them that he needed to live his life again without someone always watching over his shoulder. Bradley seemed upset by David's frank but fair words about the way his life had been since Mike Reese was killed.

"I know that you want to keep me safe and I love all of you for that, but sometimes you just have to live or life will pass you by", David said. "I will call just as soon as I arrive at the store and I'll let you know when I'm done so that you will know when I'm on my way home again okay." "But trust me when I say I have to live or I will die."

Although he could tell that, his parents didn't like his choice of words David didn't care because the most important thing was getting his message across. Bradley offered to go with him, but David said no. Not because he wished to be mean, but because he had to take this step alone.

David had only been in town about ten minutes when he thought he saw someone that looked like Mike walking across the street from where he shopped. The man had the same color hair and the same look in his eye that Mike had that day when David saw his life flash before his very eyes. Nothing had ever made him shake like that before, but now he could hear his own heartbeat in his ears.

Mike Reese is dead he told himself, but something about seeing a ghost didn't set well with the man that wanted his freedom. David called his mother so that he could hear a friendly voice, but even that didn't help much. But David didn't say anything to his mother about what he thought he saw. In fact, he told her that he was having the time of his life.

Bradley wanted to know when he thought he would be done so that he could pick him up, but David wouldn't hear of it. "Look", he said, "I drove myself and I'll get myself home again." After his little encounter with the ghost, David did his best to forget about what he thought he saw. Shopping had always been like a drug to David always putting a smile on his face, but today that wasn't happening.

Anytime someone asked how he was doing David wanted to jump out of his own skin. Fear had started to take over his soul the way that Mike and Sara tried to take his life away before. Bradley had been right about the fact that he wasn't ready to be alone just yet, but David wasn't telling anyone that he wasn't ready. Once everything was packed in the car that afternoon David called his mother to let her know that he was on his way home, but that would be the last time anyone heard from David Williams.

The hours passed and there was no sign of David anywhere. Amanda and Charles had called the police several times before they told Bradley about him missing. Once Bradley heard the words David's gone Fear took over and the young detective was on the phone making sure that everyone was looking for David.

Although he hadn't been missing for twenty-four hours Bradley didn't care and since he was a part of the Richmond Police Department, everyone was willing to overlook the fact that only a few hours had passed.

§

David couldn't understand what had just happened, but he knew that his head hurt like crazy. The room he was in looked dark as night, but when he called out no one answered. "Hello", David said hoping to hear a friendly voice, but the man that spoke back took the breath right out of him. David knew right away that the man was Mike Reese. But before he could ask the burning question, Mike told him that when you want something bad enough you do what you must to survive.

Fear now filled David's body like the stars filled the night sky. "What do you want with me he asked?" But Mike refused to answer that question. "You know what I want you little bastard, so why ask?" Mike sounded cold and filled with anger as he spoke. But David couldn't help feel that he had to try and make this guy understand that he didn't have to go through with whatever he had planned with Sara.

Nothing David said made things any better, but Mike was starting to move around the room saying it will be over soon. David couldn't help but cry as he was preparing for the worst. Knowing that you're about to die doesn't make it any easier, but for David knowing made leaving this world just a little easier, because he knew that he would go to a better place.

David watched as Mike walked around in a circle asking himself when he should take David's life. Hoping that he could change his mind David tried to get Mike to talk to him, but nothing seemed to work. The man before him now was lost to all that was once human. Mike Reese had died in that fire and the man before David Williams today was nothing more than a demon from the other side.

The room was cold and damp, and David could hear cars passing them in the night, or at least it felt like night, but in truth, it was late afternoon. Mike had only been holding David for about three hours now, but to David, it felt more like days. Amanda and Charles wondered if their son would ever return home again, but Bradley Richards wondered if he would once again have to kill Mike Reese or some other sick bastard.

The hours passed like minutes and still, the family had no word about David. The police were looking all over the city hoping to find something that would tell them where David could be, but at last nothing. David in the meantime was still trying to get Mike to talk but without much success. The only thing that David understood so far is that he would die soon.

Mike seemed lost in thought every time David tried to reach him, but that didn't stop him from trying. After all, David told himself that he had nothing to lose, but everything to gain. Mike was going to kill him and he knew that, but if he could get this guy to hold off until the police arrived maybe, he would go too. David wasn't trying to live anymore, but instead take the sick ass hole with him. Mike Reese had been a victim of his own hate. Not for gay people, but for mankind its self. Somewhere along the way Mike had forgotten that people are people no matter who you sleep with, it doesn't change a thing.

Sara, on the other hand, had been hurt by her husband's bad choices, but that was no reason to kill others. Sadly for Sara, there were no second chances. Mike, on the other hand, did have a chance to do the right thing before he made that one fatal move. David had started to fill sorry for both Mike and Sara wishing that he had been able to help them see that a life without love isn't worth living. Yes, it's true that Jason should have told Sara the truth about his feelings before he slept around, but that didn't give her the right to take his life.

Mike Reese moved in closer asking David if he was ready to meet God, but David wouldn't open his mouth. Fear had taken away his ability to speak. Watching Mike move around the room like a ghost was making David feel sick, but the end would come slowly as the knife met his flesh barely breaking the skin, and it was all a game for Mike.

A body wouldn't be found for almost a week, and when the police did find it there was a message carved into the chest that read, "If I can't have you no-one can!" The police didn't know what to make of the message, but detective Bradley Richards knew what Mike meant. Amanda and Charles couldn't understand why God hated them so, as to take both of their children away. But Bradley told them that God had nothing to do with the sick bastard that did this. Although the police had no way to proving the dead body belonged to David Williams as the body had been burned and the teeth removed.

Bradley spent the next few months looking everywhere for the sick freak that took away his love. Although he and the Williams' had gone through many stages of the grieving process Bradley had come to understand that nothing David or anyone else did would change the outcome. Mike would have found a way to kill David no matter what anyone did to stop him.

Finding a killer that everyone thinks is dead isn't easy, but for Bradley Richards, it's now a way of life. Finding love in this life is hard enough without someone taking it away without just cause. David Williams had a lot of life left to live and thanks to Mike Reese, that life had been cut short, now Bradley wanted to do the same for him.

The family laid David to rest next to Sara, even though they knew in their hearts that she was just as responsible for his death as Mike Reese. After all, the two had been working together for months taking the lives of many innocent gay men without thinking twice. Mike a decorated officer of the law and Sara a beloved sister and daughter. Together they took the lives of over twenty young men. The city of Richmond may not remember them, but the Williams family will never forget.

Bradley began to heal inside, but for those that knew him, he would never be the same again. Love had come out of the darkest hour, and now it had left in that same darkness. David had been the love that was never going to come, but when it did, Bradley couldn't have been happier to find that even in a world filled with heartbreak love can still find its way into your heart.

Amanda and Charles did their best to help Bradley understand that he was now a part of their family. However, telling someone that they belong in your heart sounds easy enough, but when it comes to Bradley Richards, what sounds easy is always hard.

Bradley left the force after David's untimely death, saying that saving lives would never feel the same after losing the one he loved. David would live on in the hearts of those that knew him well, but for the rest of the world he was but another gay man killed at the hands of hatred. Mike Reese had always been odd about his feeling toward the gay men and women of Richmond but never once did Bradley think he would one day turn into a killer.

Sara Williams was the same, a sweet and loving young woman that everyone had something nice to say about. Until that night last fall when she held her brother for an hour and a half. The world was still in shock that a woman had been responsible for the deaths of so many, but David and Bradley had known the truth. Sara really did kill all those men with or without Mike.

The city of Richmond would never forget those that lost their lives at the hands of a woman that hated the world. Maybe if someone would have seen the pain that lived in her heart they could have saved her and others, but sadly, what ifs won't help now.

Bradley and the Williams family started to move forward with their lives speaking out about what they had lived through due to hate and mistrust. One man used his hate and a woman's broken heart to take the lives of over twenty people. Sara and Mike's act of violence forced the world to see what everyone wanted to forget and that's that, we are all different for a reason.

The world of sex parties has not missed a beat due to the untimely death of the young men that once attended. However, people are just a little shy about telling anything about themselves without knowing you for a while first. Even then, it's only a need to know basis. Having fun should never cost someone their life, no matter what they like sexually. Benjamin Brown and David Williams had been lovers for over fifteen years when they found themselves lost in the world of wild sex and fantasy, but that was no reason for them to die.

Bradley never wanted the world to forget his beloved, but not because he was a gay man, but because he deserved nothing less. Benjamin was only thirty-two years old at the time of his death. And David, just thirty-one at his. Mr. and Mrs. Williams wanted to understand why they had to lose both of their children even though they didn't understand why Sara did the things that she did, they only knew that they loved their daughter.

Maybe no one will ever understand the tragedy that befell the city of Richmond, but one thing is for sure, people will never forget Sara Williams and Mike Reese. The two of them had taken the lives of more than twenty young gay men in the matter of a few months, and they have left a city filled with unanswered questions that would haunt the living for years to come.

Bradley Richards wanted to make the pain that now filled his soul leave, but he didn't know how. Amanda and Charles Williams wanted to feel whole again even if it lasted but a day. And the city of Richmond wanted to know that nothing like that would ever happen again! In the end, no one ever seems to get what they want.

The road seemed empty as darkness began to overcome. The only thing visible on the highway a set of headlights going nowhere, or so it seemed, but the man behind the wheel had his plan. The young victim in the trunk was coming to, awakening from a sleep that seemed to last for hours. The young man's fate was unknown, but he prayed for life. The man behind the wheel began to smile as the ideas danced around his head. This one was special, and maybe, just maybe, he would keep him alive.

Words of Thanks

As always I have to thank God, for giving me the words. I also have to thank my family for their love and understanding. I know that I am hard to live with while I work. Please forgive the long hours and endless typing. Just know that I love you, and I will stop working too much someday.

Over the years I have found myself lost in the world of fiction, and I have to say, I love it. Writing saved my life more than once, and I'm very grateful for the gift. Truly, I was blessed when the father opened my eyes to show me what I could do.

I also need to thank my late mother for forcing me to think about something besides love..... She was right; I can write anything my heart desires. I hope that you find something that makes you smile and simply enjoy. Writing has become the great passion of my life. Find your passion, and live your dreams only then will you find true happiness.

Happy Reading,

_J. D._

For more information about this author:
  www.JDWilld.com

www.authorjdwilld.blogspot.com

Share your thoughts about this and all of my works with me at.
jd@jdwilld.com

www.ingramcontent.com/pod-product-compliance
Lightning Source LLC
Chambersburg PA
CBHW020206270626
47157CB00028B/1549